For fourteen years now *Perry Rhodan*
has been acknowledged to be the world's
top-selling science fiction series.
Originally published in magazine form in
Germany, the series has now appeared in
hardback and paperback in the States.

Over five hundred *Perry Rhodan* clubs
exist on the Continent and *Perry Rhodan*
fan conventions are held annually. The
first Perry Rhodan film, *SOS From Outer
Space*, has now been released in Europe.

The series has sold over 140 million copies
in Europe alone.

Also available in the *Perry Rhodan* series

Clark Darlton

PERRY RHODAN 20:

The Thrall of Hypno

Futura Publications Limited
An Orbit Book

An Orbit book

First published in Great Britain in 1976
by Futura Publications Limited
Copyright © 1972 by Ace Books

An Ace Book, arrangement with Arthur Moewig Verlag
This series was created by Karl-Herbert Scheer and
Walter Ernsting, Translated by Wendayne Ackerman
and edited by Forrest J Ackerman and Frederik Pohl.
'Pursuit to Mars', originally copyrighted as 'Edison's
Conquest of Mars'; revised and edited version
copyrighted 1969, 1972 by Forrest J Ackerman.
H G Wells Interview (Scientifilm World) copyright 1936
by Julius Schwartz; by permission of Mr Schwartz.
'Things to Come' photos copyright 1936 by London
Films & United Artists.

The characters in this book are imaginary, although
the incidents depicted are largely based on fact.

ISBN: 0 8600 7924 4

Printed in Great Britain by
Richard Clay (The Chaucer Press), Ltd., Bungay, Suffolk

Futura Publications Limited
110 Warner Road, Camberwell, London SE5

This English Edition is dedicated to the late
HENRY KUTTNER and all his Pseudonyms.
Hank *must* have been a mutant to have produced so
prodigiously and well in his all-too-brief Earthspan.

1 CAPTIVE MINDS

MARS.

An uninhabited planet. At least, no intelligent life was indigenous to this world. A primitive vegetation clung precariously to life there in the low-lying belts and on the flat slopes of the hills. Insects and small mammals lived in the deserts. But none of these were a danger to man.

Something on Mars, however, seemingly was.

All tracks appeared to lead to the Red Planet. All tracks of the criminal mastermind, Monterny. The Super-mutant. The Mutant Master.

Piloting the *Good Hope VII*, Major Deringhouse of the New Power stared down through narrowed eyes at the endless red desert crisscrossed by wide green belts at curiously regular intervals. Nothing – no trace of the elusive enemy. And so, sighing, the major altered the course of his spaceship so that it soared upward till Mars diminished to a reddish globe sinking into the depths of space.

The spherical spaceship shot past Phobos, moon of Mars, out into the interplanetary void.

At incredible speed, Deringhouse raced toward his pre-arranged destination in the 200-foot diameter ship. The crew of fifteen were almost lost inside the great vessel of the void yet no more men were needed to operate the rocket for virtually every operation was performed automatically.

In the big berths of the giant ship was room for ten of the newest space-interceptors, each carrying three men and capable of light-speed. It was to a rendezvous with these ten interceptors that Deringhouse sped.

The major wasn't at all certain that he would find the menacing Supermutant on Mars. Although his trail *seemed* to lead to the Red Planet, the Solar system was wide and deep and there were still many unexplored planets where one could find refuge and dig in comfortably with the aid of adequate technical equipment. There was no *compelling* reason why it had to be Mars.

Deringhouse watched the disappearing planet on the rear viewscreen. The commander was alone in the control cabin of his spaceship and had a little time to spare. In ten minutes automatic deceleration would take effect and guide the ship to the proper coordinates. Perhaps the interceptors were already there, waiting for him, but for understandable reasons they preferred not to communicate by radio.

The major fell to musing. The Supermutant – 'the most dangerous man in the Solar system!' How exaggerated that sounded. But Deringhouse knew the description was not stretching the truth. Clifford Monterny was in fact a mutant extraordinary. Son of a formerly well-known scientist who had been caught in the radiation of an atomic reactor gone wild, the father's genetic constitution had been altered so that when Clifford was born he was not as other children. Although his difference was not at once apparent, bit by bit his unusual abilities began to make themselves manifest. He was a hypno and suggestor whose Svengali power held in thrall anyone he chose, had he met them but once, though they might be on the other side of the globe. When these abilities were finally augmented by telepathy, his three supranormal gifts, native intelligence and fortune inherited from his father gained him access to the most influential circles.

Physically, Monterny was not a very prepossessing personality. His puffy face and premature baldness didn't help much to entice people to crave his company. Perhaps these conditions contributed to the forming of his character.

Clifford Monterny was a mutant and he knew that more mutants existed on Earth. Perry Rhodan even commanded a Mutant Corps that enabled him to create his own autonomous country. Why should he idly stand by while others acted?

His talents made it possible for him to find thirteen mutants and to bring them under his mental control. With them he opened his campaign against his greatest adversary, against Perry Rhodan.

Major Deringhouse grinned broadly. He stretched his long body and yawned heartily.

Well, here the clever Supermutant had committed a blunder. It wasn't that easy to outsmart Perry Rhodan, especially if he attempted to beat him with his own weapons.

Monterny had left his mutants in the lurch and fled with a stolen spaceship. And now Major Deringhouse was hunting for the fugitive on orders from Perry Rhodan. The search had already lasted four weeks — without the slightest success.

He looked once more at the observation screen. Mars had become a bright star that shimmered like a reddish eye in the eternal night. The two moons were no longer visible. Deringhouse sighed and turned his attention to the forward observation screen. As radio communications were only advisable in case of emergency, he depended solely on optical sensors for his contact with the ten interceptors.

Deringhouse worried that Perry Rhodan wouldn't be very happy with the result of his mission to date. It was just as well that Rhodan was so busy on Terra that he didn't have time to bother him. Maybe he would get lucky and ...

A bright flash distracted him from his speculations. His skilled hands quickly manipulated the controls of the optical sensor. The three-dimensional picture of empty space vanished from the screen, black and white blotches swirled around, arranged themselves and became a new picture. There were fewer stars in view. No other change except the flashes. They were closer and clearer. And so it remained. One of the interceptors had arived.

Half an hour later nine of the smaller spaceships had returned into the gigantic hull of *Good Hope VII*. Deringhouse called their commanders to the Command center and asked for their reports. 'Lieutenant Hill, you were assigned to observe sector BNZ. What have you noticed?'

A young man wearing the uniform of the New Power stepped forward and saluted smartly. His eager face did not conceal his disappointment. 'Commander of interceptor Z-VII-1, Lieutenant Hill. We observed nothing unusual, sir. We patrolled the sector as ordered with special attention to radio signals. None were received. Same negative results from optical sensors. That's all, sir.'

'Commander Z-VII-7, Captain Berner. I've nothing irregular to report. We passed a shower of meteors at safe distance.'

The other reports revealed just as little. When the commander of the ninth interceptor finished his statement, Deringhouse glanced at the observation screen, shaking his head. 'What's keeping Z-VII-3?' he asked. 'It should've been back long ago.'

He received no answer. The Z-VII 3 was missing and never heard from again.

* * *

Sergeant Raab was terribly bored. These endless patrol flights got on his nerves since they had already gone on for four weeks. Who knew where that infamous Supermutant was hiding or whether he still existed. Every corner on Mars had been investigated and the two little moons had not been overlooked, nor had they failed to methodically patrol the interplanetary space between Mars and the asteroid belt. Nowhere was anything discovered.

Today's assignment led the craft back once again to the close proximity of the red planet. A landing had not been scheduled. Lieutenant Yomo, the Japanese commander of the Z-VII-3, shared his Sergeant's lack if interest and the third man of the team, Cadet Fowler, apparently chose not to express the same feelings, being the lowest-ranking member of the crew.

'How about Deimos?' Raab growled, looking at the irregular mass of rocks. 'It's impossible for a ship to hide there and if I correctly remember the information we were given, the Supermutant still has got two of the interceptors he stole from Rhodan.'

'I quite agree with you, sergeant,' Yomo admitted. He was one of those officers who considered the opinions of his subordinates. 'Nevertheless we'll have to investigate it. Orders seldom seem to make sense. Cadet Fowler, circle Deimos at a safe distance. Sergeant Raab, you watch the surface of the moon while I take care of the optical sensor so that we won't miss anything.'

If Lieutenant Yomo had taken his duties a little more seriously, he would have lived an hour later. But how was he to know? No one else had been able to foresee it.

That Deimos was empty was plain to see after they had passed only three times around it. The rugged rocks on the dwarf of a moon without atmosphere threw sharply contrasting shadows despite the fact that the Sun was far away and gave little light or warmth. The almost ten-mile-big heap of rocks orbited around Mars in about thirty hours at a distance of approximately 12,000 miles.

Sergeant Raab shook his head and finally said: 'It's no use holding a six-day race here all by ourselves. We'll never catch up with ourselves anyway. Not even a mouse could hide down there on that desolate rock.'

'I'm with you,' Lieutenant Yomo assented. 'Cadet Fowler, change your course to Phobos.'

'That makes it worse,' Raab groaned. 'That miserable clump is even smaller.'

'Orders are orders,' Yomo replied firmly and turned back to his instruments. 'Fowler, change course as directed.'

The trim interceptor went off on a tangent and shot straight toward Mars. Phobos was only about 4000 miles away from its planet and completed its path in a few hours. Its trajectory resembled that of an artificial satellite but it was in this respect no different from other moons. Earlier theories to that effect proposed by some scientists on Earth were not confirmed. Phobos was a natural body like Deimos and it proved to be no more interesting for the three on the Z VII-9.

Nothing.

It had been ever the same for the last four weeks and presumably was to remain the same in the coming four weeks.

Lieutenant Yomo looked at his watch. 'We still have time to go quickly around Mars. Although Major Deringhouse is searching the same territory today, I don't think we'll run into him. Better too much than not enough.'

The interceptor slipped with drastically throttled speed into the thin atmosphere, sank lower and glided at low altitude across the barren desert.

Sergeant Raab shook his head and said to Cadet Fowler: 'It doesn't matter how low we go down, I don't believe we'll find anything. The Supermutant isn't dumb enough to put on an exhibition of his stolen ships for us. If anything, he'll hide out in the asteroid belt. You want to bet?'

'I never bet,' Fowler evaded. 'But if you like, I'll

gladly agree with you.'

Raab muttered something incomprehensible and looked at Lieutenant Yomo. The Japanese nodded.

'We'll take one more quick look at those foothills over there. Then it'll be time to start back. Major Deringhouse doesn't like it very much if we're late.'

Sergeant Raab began to notice something peculiar going on when the Z-VII-3 crossed the mountain ridge and approached the plateau lying behind it. He felt as if a ring of iron had encircled his forehead and was squeezing it. Something seemed to reach for his brain. Before he was able to grasp what it meant, Yomo shouted: 'Helmets! Quick!'

He was still speaking as he pulled out an odd-looking contraption from a compartment and clapped it on his head. It resembled a crash helmet covered with wire mesh. Two little metallic rods were fastened to the frontal side. It was specially constructed to protect the human brain against hypnotic mental vibrations.

After Sergeant Raab donned his helmet he felt immediate relief. The pressure in his head subsided. Cadet Fowler felt exactly the same sensation.

But little did they know that this very same fact sealed their fate.

Somewhere under the mesa was the lair of the Supermutant from where he endeavoured with his formidable powers to bring the crew of the Z-VII-3 under his hypnotic control. When he failed to accomplish this, due to their precaution of quickly grabbing their helmets and putting them on their heads, he intended to make sure that the three men would never be in a position to betray his hide-out.

It happened instantaneously.

One moment the trim interceptor was floating slowly over the trackless mountains of Mars to detect the cause of the sudden attempt at mind capture – and the next moment the cockpit of the craft exploded in a flaming blast. The atomic terror engulfed the ship with one stroke and swallowed it up. Half molten debris plummeted crazily down and smashed onto the rocks below. A cloud of smoke lazily drifted eastward in the gentle breeze.

And it was all over.

*　　　*　　　*

When the interceptor Z-VII-3 failed to show up at the rendezvous after four hours, Major Deringhouse lost his patience. He asked the commanders of the interceptors once more to come to the Command Center. The customary smile on his lips was gone. His face looked serious and stern.

'Gentlemen, the failure of Lieutenant Yomo to return permits a number of conclusions and we can choose one of them.'

The commanders waited tensely. They knew that Deringhouse had no pleasant alternatives to outline for them.

'Z-VII-3 has found the hiding place of the Supermutant and was captured or destroyed in the encounter. If only the first had occurred, we should've received a radio call from him as he was instructed to do. There is also the possibility that Lieutenant has become a victim of a malfunction of his craft. And, thirdly, he could've been hit by a meteor.'

Lieutenant Hill cleared his throat. Deringhouse looked at him questioningly. 'Perhaps things arcn't as black as they appear,' said Hill, 'and Lieutenant Yomo has only been delayed. Which sector did he have to patrol today?'

Deringhouse shook his head. 'I'm inclined to rule this out. It was Lieutenant Yomo's task to explore Mars and its vicinity. I was there myself with the *Good Hope VI* but didn't see anything that was suspicious. Since we must assume that the Supermutant has flown to Mars, thc absence of Lieutenant Yomo raises extremely grave doubts. I must admit that I'm greatly worried.'

'Why don't we take a look ourselves?' somebody asked.

Deringhouse looked in the direction of the speaker. 'Isn't that what we've been doing for four weeks?'

'Certainly, Major. But if your first assertion regarding the Z-VII-3 is correct, Lieutenant Yomo must have unearthed something. If the Supermutant is actually on Mars, he is bound to have an adequate refuge. Perhaps Yomo has detected it by accident. We don't know what happened subsequently but we can try to check up on it.'

'If I understand you correctly you propose a more intensive inspection of Mars?'

'Right, sir!'

Deringhouse glanced at the other officers. 'And what do you think, gentlemen?'

'It sounds like a good idea,' commented Captain Berger. 'At any rate, it's better than sitting here idly.'

Deringhouse deliberated for a few seconds and then the old smile flitted again across his face. 'Ready for action in ten minutes! Crews to man interceptors! Ship out at once.'

The commanders of the little fighting ships saluted and left the Command Center. Deringhouse watched till they were gone. Then he stopped smiling and sat down in the seat before the controls. He waited five more minutes before he switched on the intercom. Lieutenant Hill reported:

'Hangar one ready. Nine interceptors set for launching.'

'All right,' Deringhouse replied, glancing at the map of coordinates lying before him. 'The airlock will be opened in two minutes. Take off at once and stay close to the guppy during flight. Is that clear?'

'Perfectly,' Hill acknowledged.

A minute and a half after this short exchange a panel slid back in the hull of the huge spaceship and created an opening. Illuminated by bright lights the little agile interceptors stood on the starting ramps inside the hangars. The first one started to move abruptly and shot with awesome acceleration out into free space. Before it could curve around it was already followed by the next one. The entire operation lasted less than two minutes. The light in the hangars went dark and the hatch closed up again. *Good Hope VII* began to accelerate. The interceptors coordinated their speeds and took the mothership into their midst in an orderly formation. Far out in front of them among the multitudinous swarm of cold shining stars stood a shimmering reddish light – Mars. The polar caps and the web of canals stood clearly out from the monotonous flat desert.

With an expressionless face Major Deringhouse looked at his destination.

He began to sense that a terrible fate was awaiting him.

*   *   *

The hall was deep below the surface.

The walls consisted of rough-hewn rocks, the ceiling was bare and the floor was covered with a synthetic carpet. Glaring lamps illuminated the room with an unpleasant light. The occupant of the subterranean cavern didn't seem to care much for comfort. One of the naked walls was almost hidden by an array of various technical instruments. Cables and conduits were strung in a tangled mess on the floor and led through a small opening into an adjacent room. The hum of a working reactor could be heard somewhere, otherwise everything was quiet.

The air in the room was good with a typical synthetic freshness similar to that inside a spaceship. High above on the ceiling the whirring of a ventilator was audible.

The unbearable light went out. For a moment it seemed to be pitchdark. Then a picture screen on a wall lit up spreading a cold but mild shine. A table and a control panel became discernible in the semi-darkness.

A man was sitting on a chair before the table. He wore a simple dark-gray business suit. His bald and massive skull was shining in the dim light of the picture screen. The puffy face was only vaguely recognizable. He had big cold eyes, ears that were much too small and thick lips that were pressed hard together.

His head sat on a short fat neck. His bulky body rested on a sturdy steel chair that had apparently been removed from a spaceship. He stretched his muscular legs under the table and his chubby hands were lying motionlessly on the table before the controls.

Clifford Monterny, the Supermutant, formerly master of thirteen mutants who threatened under his command to break Perry Rhodan's power until they were defeated and liberated by the man they attacked. Clifford Monterny, the greatest enemy of Terra and the most dangerous man in the solar system, was holed up below the surface of Mars and waiting for his chance.

He was still in possession of two of the three stolen interceptors. It was much too little to conduct a war against the Earth. He needed more ships and more men. Once they came under the spell of his powerful hypnotic will, they were bound to obey his orders blindly. Naturally it was a difficult feat to influence unknown persons over great distances but he knew from experience that it was not impossible. This was the purpose of the observation screen in his hide-out. The image of a face on the videoscreen was sufficient to recognize the brain-wave pattern of the person and that was all he needed to take over his mind.

A change became noticeable on the screen. The colors became blurred and rearranged themselves. The glittering of the stars was extinguished by the shadow of a gigantic metalic sphere. For a moment it looked as if a round hole had appeared in the universe. Soon the picture was finely focused and it reflected plastically *Good Hope VII* in its full size.

The Supermutant adjusted the picture again. Now it showed only a section of the vessel but there wasn't much he could do with that either. It was necessary to see a face in order to insure a hundred percent success. A partial success was liable to backfire. If the crew of the big ship became aware too soon of his mental intrusion and put on their insolation helmets, he would be rendered ineffective and forced to destroy the spaceship which he needed so badly to put his plans into action.

The commander of the main battleship should be led to assume that the Supermutant had no other desire than to demolish his ship. In order to create this diversionary delusion it was indispensable that he destroyed some of the accompanying interceptors.

Once again the Supermutant changed the picture. The formation of the nine interceptors replaced the spacesphere.

The Supermutant watched them though narrow eyes. His lips were distorted in a malicious grin. If those poor devils only know how helpless they were against him in their little ships, they would turn tail and scramble away with the speed of light anywhere at all. Alas, they didn't know.

Nobody knew about the dreadful weapon he could wield!

He congratulated himself on his foresight that he established his base on Mars even before he declared war on Rhodan and he was particularly proud to have brought Ivan Goratschin to Mars, his mightiest and most awesome weapon against which no defense existed!

He looked at the control scale underneath the videoscreen. The hostile fleet was still 12,000 miles away. Since its velocity was steadily decreasing it would take another ten minutes to reach the Martian atmosphere, time enough to make the necessary preparations.

Clifford Monterny, the human monster, wondered for a few seconds whether the other pilots knew about the annihilation of the interceptor or whether it was just a pure accident that they approached his secret refuge.

He threw a last glance at the observation screen before he lifted his corpulent body out of the chair and went to the door. He locked it carefully after leaving the room and walked with short quick steps down the long hallway lined on both sides with more doors.

Finally he stopped and touched a magnetic lock, making a metallic panel slide back into the rock. Through the opening he stepped into the room behind.

The room was almost empty of furniture except for the barest necessities. A bed stood in the corner opposite the door.

And somebody was sitting on that bed ...

The horrible sight was enough to make one's blood freeze in its veins but the Supermutant merely smiled and said: 'Get up and come with me, Ivan. I've got work for you.'

Obediently the monster rose and followed his lord and master.

* * *

Good Hope VII descended approximately to the altitude of Phobos and went into orbit around Mars. The nine interceptors followed without special orders.

Major Deringhouse realized that from now on restricted radio communication had become indispensable. He called the radio officer on the intercom.

'Cadet Renner, call the interceptors and switch through to me.'

'Very well, sir. Which magnitude?'

'The lowest. The radio waves mustn't be allowed to penetrate to the surface of Mars.'

In less than a minute Deringhouse gave his instructions to the commanders of the interceptors. He assigned their positions and ordered them to remain in sight of each other and to conduct the sweep of the terrain together. In case anyone found the slightest clue, he was directed to notify all participants. Under no condition was anybody permitted to take off on his own. It was forbidden to use optical instruments for the time being.

Visual contact was a necessity for a concerted operation due to the extremely weak wave signals. Nobody had the slightest inkling of the real outcome of Z-VII-3's patrol flight but they had no desire to share its uncertain fate.

Z-VII-7 with Captain Berner in charge veered to the side and took its designated position. The other members of the squadron also fanned out to their respective places.

Berner left the steering to his co-pilot and concentrated on observation. He kept in constant touch with Deringhouse through his radioman.

Now the mothership departed from its circular path and commenced to get closer to the land. The interceptors did likewise and the widely staggered formation enable a thorough scrutiny of the landscape.

Captain Berner stared at the reddish plain and was prepared to swear that there was no place for the Supermutant to hide down there. Perhaps he could hole up in the mountains but never in the loose sand of the desert. Previous explorations had determined that the strata of sand reached down more than 150 feet. It was hard to imagine that anyone would bury himself down there.

'Change course to the foothills in the west,' the command came from the spacesphere. 'Go down low enough to use your telescopes. Report any sign of excavations.'

Berner strictly conformed with the instructions. Z-VII-2 was flying next to him and Z-VII-5 was farther beyond. Z-VII-4 was about to enter the thin upper atmosphere in front of him.

They were nearing the hills. The little fleet moved at low altitude across the flat slopes, hugged the crests of the mountains and crossed the shallow valleys. They hovered for a little while over one of the basins and then continued their flight.

The hills flattened out and gradually merged into

the desert. Far at the horizon another mountain came into view. Berner knew from earlier trips that this was the biggest on Mars although not the highest. The terrain gave the impression of a virtually uniform continent rising like a vast island from the ocean of the flat deserts.

What Berner couldn't know was the fact that the Supermutant considered this mountain as his private property and that he was lying in wait for the incoming fleet not very far below the cover of the bed of rocks.

Captain Berner recognized behind the first peaks the expansive plain of the mesa that he had frequently flown over before. Never had he noticed anything suspicious and he was convinced that today's search would also prove to be fruitless.

They passed a little side valley. The sparse scrubs gave way to predominately bare rocks. Still no hint of anything out of the ordinary.

Suddenly Berner closed his blinded eyes. Exactly in front of him, where the Z-VII-4 had been, a sun flamed up and dissolved the interceptor with atomic heat. Liquid metal dripped from the ball of fire and rained on the plateau. The glowing drops were trailed by plumes of smoke.

When the brilliant light faded and Berner was able to open his eyes again, there was nothing left of the Z-VII-4. In its place hovered an oddly shaped cloud that slowly drifted away in the wind.

It all had happened so fast that Berner and his co-pilot had no time to react. They kept going through to the gaseous remnants of the interceptor, tearing the cloud apart.

At the same moment a new light flared up on their left. This time Z-VII-2 fell victim to the insidious attack that struck without warning. Seconds later the Z-VII-5 also disintegrated under the assault of the invisible attacker.

At last they had caught up with the long sought adversary. However Major Deringhouse radioed instantly: 'All interceptors back to the hangar!'

The maneuver was performed with incredible speed but Z-VII-10 exploded a few feet from the safety of the hatch and the hot wave of the atomic annihilation wafted with searing heat into the hangar of *Good Hope VII*.

Five of the little fighters were finally secure again.

But they did not realize that the safety was strictly illusory. This was exactly what the Supermutant wanted.

Major Deringhouse committed a fatal blunder by disregarding the immediate protective appliction of the absorber helmets. The sudden attack on his interceptor and their inexplicable destruction, the obviously dangerously close proximity of the belligerent enemy seemed to impair his proverbial rational astuteness.

He decided to retreat.

But at the same time he made his second mistake.

The reason was understandable. He was certain that nothing could be done for the men in the demolished interceptors. Yet before he saved the Guppy and brought reinforcements from Terra he was anxious to obtain positive evidence of the whereabouts of the Supermutant. Despite the obvious fact that the *Good Hope* had been detected, nobody could seriously believe that the Supermutant was in a position to assail or damage this gigantic battleship too. The spacesphere was already shrouded in the impenetrable screen of energy.

Was it truly impenetrable?

Perhaps for all kinds of matter, even if it was shot in the form of lethal energy rays, but not for the hypnotic mental currents of the Supermutant.

Major Deringhouse committed his second error by delaying his retreat and using the optical sensor. He was determined to see the Supermutant with his own eyes as valid proof of his presence.

Motivated by the same reason he not only turned on the optical sensor but also the video transceiver.

This was the moment the Supermutant had waited for. Returning to his control room he found not only the *Good Hope* on the picture screen but he was able to stare into the face of Deringhouse.

Two seconds later the Major lost his identity.

He became a tool of the uncanny freak whose hypnotic powers took possession of his will, making his body a willing instrument of his master.

Major Deringhouse did not even sense the change himself, much less the people around him.

He switched off the optical sensor and looked at the Commanders of the remaining interceptors as they entered the Command Center. Lieutenant Hill and his five comrades saluted and waited for further instructions. These turned out to be quite different from what Hill had expected.

'We'll land on the plateau below,' Deringhouse said without hesitation. 'The refuge of the Supermutant must be somewhere around here. We can't return to Earth without results.'

Hill was unable to mask his confusion. 'But we've just lost four of our interceptors! We'll be in dreadful jeopardy!'

'Since when are we afraid of taking risks?' Deringhouse asked reproachfully. 'Our responsibility far outweighs all dangers.'

'The least we should know is the type of weapon with which our ships were attacked. Don't forget that we were protected by our defense screens.'

Deringhouse nodded gravely. 'I didn't forget it. We can't rest until we've ascertained what new weapon the Supermutant is now using. Therefore I order you to prepare for the landing. Inform the crew of the *Good Hope*. One more thing, we'll touch down and debark from the ship carrying only our breathing equipment, no weapons.

'No weapons!' Lieutenant Hill exclaimed in astonishment. 'You want to brave the Supermutant unarmed? I don't understand you.'

'It's really very simple, Lieutenant. We know that the Supermutant wields a new weapon against which even our energy shields are useless. We even have to admit the possibility that he can obliterate the *Good Hope* if he cares to do so. He chose to spare us and our last five interceptors. Why?'

Lieutenant Hill shrugged his shoulders.

Major Deringhouse permitted himself an condescending smile. 'Because he wants to show us that he is willing to negotiate with us provided we acknowledge his superiority. Well, let's formally admit that he holds the upper hand and meet him without arms. What do we have to lose under the circumstances? Nothing, Lieutenant Hill, but we've a great deal to gain under certain conditions.'

The Lieutenant had to grant that his commanding Major had some logic on his side for his opinions although they offered him no assurance whatsoever. Hill was no coward but he didn't like fighting against unknown and invisible opponents. If there was no other way he preferred to be armed to the teeth on such an occasion.

'As you say, sir,' he said finally after looking at the puzzled faces of his comrades who couldn't come up with a better answer. 'I'll pass your orders on to the crew and give them a briefing. Aren't you going to advise Terra of your decision?'

Major Deringhouse quickly shook his head, maybe a little too quickly. But then, who would notice it? 'That would be a mistake, possibly a disastrous mistake. The Supermutant must be lulled into thinking that no risks are involved. If he overhears our radio message he'll find out that we plan to dupe him and that it is merely a pretext if we agree to his conditions. You must leave now, Lieutenant. We've got no time to lose.'

Forty men followed Deringhouse's orders with mixed feelings. They knew their commander as an audacious yet cautious man who was loath to taking unnecessary chances. This time however he seemed to underestimate the perils. The Supermutant was also a telepath and was able to read their thoughts. He would learn that they came totally disarmed despite the fact that they were enemies. How would this change the situation? Most likely not at all.

Good Hope VII slowly descended toward the plateau, passed over it at low altitude and finally touched down near a rocky outcropping that rose like a sugar-loaf from the stony plain.

Major Deringhouse shifted all controls to the stand-still position, stared a few seconds with a vacant expression at the dimmed observation screens and switched on the intercom. Everyone on board listened to what he had to say.

'I'm going to leave the ship with ten men to meet the Supermutant. Five of the Guppy's officers and the five commanders of the interceptors will accompany me. Smith will take over command of the *Good Hope* during my absence. No radio communication with Terra will be permitted and incoming calls may not be answered. Is that clear?'

From the radio room came a confirmation that sounded very baffled. None of the other departments professed much enthusiasm. The feeling of surrendering helplessly to a sworn enemy was deeply resented. Somehow it was not compatible with Deringhouse's personality.

Ten minutes later the exit hatch opened and Deringhouse was the first one to step on the ground of the red planet followed by the ten officers. All wore light protective suits and the necessary breathing masks. None of them carried arms.

'There,' said Deringhouse pointing to the rocky

cone, 'is the entrance to the hiding place of the Super-mutant.' Without waiting for an answer he started to walk.

Lieutenant Hill stood still and rubbed his eyes.

'How do you know, sir, that this is the secret place we've been trying to find for weeks? I think you owe us an explanation.'

The pressure on his brain increased. He saw that Berner touched his head too and mumbled something incomprehensible. The breathing mask made understanding impossible.

He was seized by a horrible suspicion but before he could utter a warning cry it was already too late.

Suddenly he became very calm.

With a steadfast stride he followed behind Dering-house, who paid no attention to his men but did what the Supermutant ordered him to do. Him and his ten officers!

2　THE ULTIMATE WEAPON

Much had happened on Terra during the past few weeks.

Perry Rhodan had tackled the task of creating a world government with all available means. He commanded enough power to establish it since the inexhaustible resources of the Arkonides were at his disposal. The humanoides he had rescued on the Moon had refrained in the last months from repeating their continual demands, well-known to Rhodan, for the return to their home. The planet Arkon was 34,000 light-years away from Earth, a distance that could easily be covered by the starship *Stardust II*. However Rhodan had urgent reasons to postpone the homeward journey for Khrest and Thora time and time again. He was unalterably opposed to the discovery of the Earth's existence by Arkon for fear that the empire was bent on incorporating Terra. Only after Terra was united and strong would the way be paved for opening relations.

He was unable to delay the inevitable contact much longer unless he completely alienated the two Arkonides whom he owed so much. This was the main reason behind his strenuous efforts to install the united world government as soon as possible.

Extraordinary diplomatic activities took place in Terrania to achieve this purpose. After the initial consultations with the presidents of the international power blocs their representatives were conferring in the capital of the New Power, as Rhodan's state in the former Gobi Desert was called. Terrania was the most modern city on the globe. It had a population of one and a half million inhabitants, a farflung spaceport and an army of 10,000 soldiers as well as robot fighters of Arkonide and Terranian construction.

Its central installations were permanently covered by a tremendous energy dome which had already withstood atomic attacks.

Perry Rhodan took an elevator up to the top floor of the Security Ministry where Reginald Bell, Chief of the Ministry, conducted a debate among the representatives of the three major world powers.

Rhodan entered without announcement, gave a friendly greeting to Bell and the other delegates and took a chair. He had no intention of intervening in the debate but he wanted to take a first hand look at the progress of the negotiations.

Security Minister Bell returned the glance of his friend Rhodan. Bell had a glow in his eyes.

He turned to the members of the conference. The representative of the Asiatic Federation, a corpulent Chinese, glanced sideways at his neighbor, the American emissary from the Western Bloc before he fired his next question:

'The preparations for the world-wide elections are under way, Mister Bell, but I must honestly confess that I have my doubts about the success of this inspiring undertaking and I'm afraid that the informative programs of your television stations won't change the state of affairs. Our generation is too much imbued with the spirit of nationalism.'

'Do you mean to say,' Bell leaned forward and looked questioningly at the Chinese, 'that mankind is not interested in an accord?'

'I've claimed no such thing,' the other defended himself against the accusation. 'I've merely pointed out some of the difficulties. I'm convinced that my two colleagues will agree with me that these difficulties are prevalent.'

The representative of the Eastern Bloc nodded affirmatively.

'Despite the rejection of nationalism we've practiced for five decades, it is deeply rooted in the people and it comes to the fore when you need it least. I must admit that there is opposition to the idea of world government in our ranks. The election will simply be ignored by some of these people.'

Bell looked at the American. The elderly delegate cleared his throat and stated:

'The allies of the Western Bloc used to call themselves the free world. Of course we've refused to stamp out nationalism by force. It was supposed to fade away. There are voices in our countries too that disapprove of a world government because they fear a domineering tutelage from those quarters.'

The two other representatives made signs of agreement which were duly noted with interest by Perry Rhodan who kept in the background. Reginald Bell restrained himself with a shrug of his shoulders.

'The government heads of the three power blocs

have unanimously agreed that only a world government will be able to cope with a future impasse. Irrespective of these problems, every man on Earth will eventually have to come to grips with the fact that we're not the only intelligent inhabitants of the universe. A few light-years away from us flourish realms of stars comprising many solar systems. Compared to their size and might we're like a single family compared to the power of a big government. Families cannot exist for long on their own and neither can Terra if torn by internecine strife in the cosmic age. The first conqueror who discovers Earth will incorporate it in his empire.'

He stopped speaking. Before his eyes the events of the last four weeks rolled by again. While the little fleet under Major Deringhouse tried to catch the Supermutant who had fled, the preparation for the most important and all-inclusive elections that had ever taken place on Terra had commenced. All mankind was to decide on what to choose – national governments or a world government. For years already artificial satellites provided television reception at every point of the globe. This made possible an unprecedented worldwide propaganda campaign with thorough indoctrination. Day and night, films produced by the New Power were shown all over the world. Robot-controlled simultaneous translation machines spoke the explanatory text.

These films depicted the attacks from intelligent forces in space on peaceful and unprepared worlds and their destruction. They related again the story of the reptilian Topides who attempted to conquer the Ferronian people in the Vega system. Only with the help of Perry Rhodan had the unfortunate Ferronians been able to repulse the invaders from their world.

In harsh terms the New Power endeavored to inform all people what would happen to them if they insisted on their narrow-minded attitude.

Perry Rhodan was almost continually on the road himself, making election trips. He made speeches on television stations all over the world, expounding the great mission of a united mankind that would reach far beyond the Solar system. He reminded his listeners that contact with the Arkonides was imminent and that the existence of Terra was imperilled if that far-advanced race should determine that the Earth's citizens still failed to live up to their destiny. The Arkonides, he stressed, were not prepared to deal as equals with backward people. Earth would just become another colony in their vast empire.

Reginald Bell did not remember that Rhodan had spoken before so frankly about mankind's destiny but those who could read between the lines began to understand what he failed to mention. The Arkonides, Perry Rhodan implied, were, in spite of their incredible civilization and superb technical achievements, a decadent race. One day they would be compelled to step down and a successor had to be found for the majestic empire of stars. And if Terra by that time ...

The idea was too far out to think it through to the end.

Reginald Bell turned to the representative of the Eastern Bloc.

'Did you wish to make a comment? Please go ahead!'

'Our nations believe that the world government will be secretly dominated by Perry Rhodan. They object to living under a dictatorship just when we've begun to liberate ourselves.'

Rhodan smiled mildly, rose up and stepped forward. Then he addressed the man from the Eastern Bloc:

'Such misgivings can be easily dispelled with a little logic. You know as well as I do that the New Power is militarily in a position to impose the world government against the will of all countries. However, we wouldn't think of using force. Only voluntary adherence to a common goal will make us strong. History has taught us that force breeds counterforce and downfall. Don't entertain the idea that I advocate unconditional pacifism – this wouldn't get us anywhere either. I merely consider both extremes as counterproductive and detrimental.'

'All right,' the delegate from the Eastern Bloc replied. 'I'm willing to believe you personally but what measures can we take to convince all our people?'

Rhodan smiled.

'We can resort to a time-honored custom for this purpose. You can invite me for an official state visit and I'll come with the Arkonide battleship and an army of robots. Don't you think that such a spectacle would be very impressive?'

'It could be interpreted as an attempt at intimidation, sir.'

'That's just what it's meant to be,' Rhodan admitted bluntly. 'Those people with closed minds might be persuaded by their own eyes with such a demonstration.'

Reginald Bell suppressed a grin. This diplomatic sparring amused him royally and it was much more entertaining than the fruitless attempts of chasing the Supermutant. He knew better than anybody else the infinite patience Rhodan practiced to refrain from achieving his goal with more energetic means. By taking advantage of the military superiority of the Arkonide weapons he could have conquered the Earth in a few hours. However he was not out to conquer the world, he wanted to win the hearts of all its people. For it is a strange yet wise principle of nature that only a free man can accomplish truly great deeds.

The representative of the Asiatic Federation smiled cryptically and leaned forward, saying: 'Isn't it possible to have a united Earth with sovereign governments of independent power blocs? Peace could be guaranteed by mutual treaties.'

Rhodan smiled back with a trace of coldness. 'Is that what you think? We all know from history that treaties are made to be broken. No, this is no solution. We need a competent government that is ready to act at a moment's notice. In a crucial emergency there won't be time to consult legislatures and parliaments. Our planet has to confront intelligent aliens as one formidable undivided unit. World bodies lacking a unified government that reflects basically coordinated thinking, are considered according to interstellar laws as retrogressive and are treated harshly. Would you let this happen to us?'

The Chinese had listened attentively and shook his head. 'As far as I'm concerned I fully share your opinion. I've merely cited the arguments of the dissenters. You stated yourself that contrasting views will have to be reconciled.'

'It's our duty to be fair,' Rhodan admitted. 'But a weak world government carries its own seed of destruction from the beginning. Besides, I keep asking myself in vain, why would a reasonable man object to the harmonious cooperation of mankind?'

Reginald Bell cleared his throat. 'That's simple,' he said, 'if you know human character. Naturally nobody is going to object to unity and world government as long as he can pull the strings himself. But everybody resists that same collaboration if someone else has the authority, or to phrase it differently, no person wants the other to rule and be relegated to a subordinate position.'

'Not even if it benefits mankind?' Rhodan ruminated.

'Not even then,' Bell insisted.

The representatives of the three big powers looked terribly disconsolate for awhile.

* * *

A short time later an internal conference took place, attended by the closest assistants of Rhodan.

When Perry Rhodan entered the room he glanced at his assembled co-workers and assured himself that all those invited were present.

Colonel Freyt, his official deputy, was standing next to the Arkonide Khrest, whose tall figure towered above all the others. The white hair, the high forehead and the reddish albino eyes marked him as a member of the race that ruled an empire 34,000 light-years away – or believed that it still ruled.

Thora and Bell stood closeby. Thora was also very tall and had the same hair and eyes as Khrest. She was an exquisite beauty. She spoke softly to Bell but fell silent the moment Rhodan entered the room. She paid no further attention to Bell but followed every movement of Rhodan with her inquisitive eyes.

John Marshall took part as representative of the Mutant Corps. The Australian telepath had no trouble reading the thoughts of everybody in the room but didn't care to take the trouble. He belonged to the generation whose parents were exposed to the effects of the early atomic explosions. Now there was one mutant per million people. However only rarely had the changes been for the better.

In one corner Dr. Manoli and Dr. Haggard argued about the best method for the prevention of space sickness, which still occurred occasionally. Their discussion ended as soon as they noticed Rhodan coming in.

Reginald Bell excused himself from Thora and walked toward Rhodan. He planted himself three steps in front of Rhodan and reported: 'Top echelon of New Power present for routine consultation, sir.'

Rhodan smiled indulgently. 'Thank you, Bell. In future you may save yourself that "sir." Good evening, friends. I thank you for coming. We want to make it short. On my part, I don't have much to tell.

The negotiations with the three world powers have yet to produce positive results. I'm afraid it'll be a long time before we can expect them to reach concrete conclusions. That's about the extent of my report.'

Thora cast a glance at Khrest but the Arkonide shook his head almost unnoticeably. John Marshall, the telepath, smiled knowingly. Thora wanted to ask Rhodan again when he intended at last to take Khrest and her back to Arkon. This question had become a routine – just like Rhodan's negative answer.

Colonel Freyt caught Rhodan's questioning look. He stepped in front of Khrest, with whom he had been standing, and said: 'We had maintained visual contact with *Good Hope VII* through the relay station ship Z-45 although we had no personal contact with Major Deringhouse. Yesterday we observed nine interceptors flying in battle formation with the *Guppy VII* toward Mars. At this point we lost our visual contact as the Z-45 couldn't dare to get closer.'

This was certainly disconcerting news. Rhodan asked Colonel Freyt: 'Have you instructed the Z-45 to watch the situation closely?'

'Of course, sir. I'm expecting a report any moment. The radio officer in charge has orders to inform me as soon as we receive it.'

'All right, Freyt. I'm afraid our trouble with the Supermutant is far from over. It's too bad I have to conduct the negotiations with the governments myself and have to prepare and supervise the world elections. Otherwise I could pay more attention to the action against the Supermutant. Perhaps Bell can attend to this matter in my place if the situation calls for it.'

Bell's face looked resentful and he warded the suggestion off with a gesture. 'Perhaps you remember, Perry, that five weeks ago I roamed the universe for days to track down that Supermutant. If I was unable to find him then, I won't have a better chance now.'

'You're making two mistakes,' Rhodan pointed out. 'In the first place there are never two identical situations – one of the factors involved has already changed. Secondly, as long as the Supermutant is alive he presents a menace to mankind such as the world has never known before. Unless we manage to eliminate this threat once and for all, our very existence will always be in jeopardy. For this you may in good conscience sacrifice a few days for an unpromising search. Unfortunately I can't leave the Earth for the moment.'

'When do you want me to start?' Bell asked exasperatedly. Rhodan failed to understand his friend's dislike for this trip into space. Normally Bell was the first one to volunteer in cases like this. Rhodan made a mental note to ask Bell for an explanation of his behaviour at a more appropriate occasion.

'It's not that urgent,' Rhodan answered. 'Let's wait first for Deringhouse's report. His instructions were to break off the search in one week if he's had no luck with it.' He changed the subject and turned to John Marshall. 'What's new in your department?'

The telepath came a few steps closer. 'The training of the eleven new mutants is making progress. The

41

poor devils don't know what's happening to them. The Supermutant robbed them of their own will and dominated their mind completely. Now they're free and can fully develop their capabilities. As far as I can determine now, the Mutant Corps has gained some new and important talents.'

'I'm going to look into this further,' Rhodan promised before he turned to Khrest. 'I hope it hasn't taken too much time to suit you. I expect very soon to be able to fulfill the promise I gave you but at the moment I've got to solve some important problems here that can't be put off. May I count on your indulgence?'

Khrest smiled benevolently but caught Thora's demanding glance. He nodded to her and said: 'I've full understanding for your dilemma, Rhodan. It is better for you to take up relations with our Imperium after Terra is unified but we can't wait forever. It's perfectly possible for you to take us to Arkon now.'

'It's not only the contact with the Arkonides that concerns me,' Rhodan stated calmly, 'and you know it as well as Thora. But consider the facts. We know that your Imperium isn't what it was 10,000 years ago. It's deteriorating and racked by revolutions. Whole solar systems are rising up against the Arkonides and are marauding and plundering throughout the universe. Two of these races have already found their way to Terra by accident. Fortunately we were able to repulse them. When we arrive at Arkon, the entire Imperium will learn the position of the Earth. A regular invasion of this rich but defenceless world would follow and we wouldn't be able to cope with so many enemies. This is the sole reason I haven't kept my promise to you so far.'

'I can see your point,' Khrest admitted, 'but we've lived voluntarily for ten years in exile, we've given you every conceivable help and you've benefitted from our knowledge and experience. Don't you think that your debt should be paid some time?'

'I fully agree with you,' Rhodan replied. 'You must trust me that I'm willing to repay you. I'll be glad to pay you back with interest.'

'Interest?' Khrest wondered.

'Yes, interest,' Rhodan nodded and smiled. 'Your realm is now going through a critical period. When we return to Arkon we'll not only have the *Stardust* but an armada of powerful battleships as well. I'll put this fleet at your disposal and promise you to restore order in the Imperium. As I see it, we can hardly expect diplomatic skills to save your nation. This leaves only reliance on a vivid demonstration of power. Your race is too old and decadent for such a show of force. Therefore, we Earthlings are going to come to your assistance and I believe that we can thus make up for our obligations.'

Khrest looked at Thora. The beautiful Arkonide woman said hesitantly: 'All right, Rhodan. We'll take your word for it. As soon as the world government has been established . . .'

'There's something else,' Rhodan interrupted. 'Let's not forget the Supermutant. Ten such monsters can conquer a solar system. Even one can imperil it seriously. He'll have to be put out of action first before . . .'

'We're willing to go along with you in this matter too,' Khrest smiled. 'I admit that the mutants are a phenomenon that is unknown to our world in this form. We've in our Imperium some lesser races whose lack of regular limbs is compensated for by their tele-kinetic capability. Nobody possesses both, as occurs on Earth. I regard this fact as a threat to the existing order.'

'It would be better to regard it as a boon to the Imperium,' Rhodan stated and looked up as the door opened and a man in the uniform of the radio personnel entered, holding a note in his hand. He stood at attention when he saw Rhodan.

'I've a message for Colonel Freyt,' he announced, saluting. 'As it seemed to be important I brought it right away.'

'Give it to me,' Colonel Freyt demanded. While he cursorily glanced at the message he knitted his brow. Although the news gave him no cause for grave concern, it appeared to make him thoughtful.

'What is it?' Rhodan asked impatiently. 'Did you hear from Deringhouse?'

Freyt looked up. 'Yes, I heard from him, although not the way I expected to. This message was sent by the relay ship Z-45 as urgent. *Guppy VII* returned from Mars and passed the Z-45 at close range without answering repeated calls. Major Deringhouse failed to react to mandatory light signals. Without slowing down he flew past the Z-45 on direct course to Terra. *Guppy VII* streaked by the Moon a few seconds ago and is approaching the government territory of the New Power in parabolic flight trajectory.'

Rhodan narrowed his eyes. 'Have we tried to make contact with him?'

Freyt nodded. 'Major Deringhouse doesn't answer, sir. Evidently he didn't switch to reception.'

'This is against regulations,' Rhodan said apprehensively. He exchanged a quick glance with Bell whose eyes brightened with concern. 'It's emergency status. Bell, inform the fleet to be ready for take-off!'

Colonel Freyt lost for a moment the aura of confidence he normally exhibited. 'Ready to start? Alarm? What's this all about?'

With unaccustomed gravity Rhodan replied: 'I've already emphasized that our security is threatened as long as the Supermutant is loose or, indeed, is alive. Don't forget that he's a hypno. Remember the mutants he mercilessly controlled for years. And if you draw the obvious conclusions, Deringhouse's strange behavior becomes a little more understandable.'

At first Bell was stunned with surprise. Then he rushed to the door. He opened it and turned around again. 'You don't seriously believe, Perry, that the Supermutant has a stranglehold on Deringhouse?'

'I'm not jumping to conclusions, Bell, but I certainly have to take such a possibility into account. Only after the Guppy has landed and John Marshall has examined the whole crew will I be satisfied. Now hurry up. Deringhouse won't keep us waiting very long.'

Khrest had turned pale and stood undecided at Thora's side. Dr. Manoli had brushed aside the problems discussed with Dr. Haggard and studied Marshall's face for an answer.

45

Rhodan turned to Colonel Freyt, advising him: 'Make sure that the radio officer calls Deringhouse constantly. Warn him that we'll open fire on him unless he answers. Put the robot fighter units on alert at the same time.'

Freyt hesitated. 'Aren't you too skeptical, sir? We might create an unnecessary disturbance. Besides, what can Deringhouse do to us, even supposing he's under the influence of the Supermutant?'

'Freyt! Carry out my instructions at once!' Rhodan said with unusual sharpness, looking angrily at his deputy. 'I've got my reasons. Better an unnecessary alarm than have the Earth destroyed. Will you please go now!'

Without another word Freyt turned around and left the room, accompanied by his radio officer.

'Manoli and Haggard,' Rhodan called the two physicians. 'Go immediately to the hospital and wait further orders.'

'But ...' Manoli began.

'What's the matter with you all? Doesn't anyone realize the danger we've to contend with. The Supermutant is the most vicious hypno that ever existed. He can have taken over Deringhouse and sent him here to trap us. Don't forget that Deringhouse ignored our radio calls. Why? You don't have any explanation for that, do you?'

The two physicians exited quietly. The remaining men looked at each other with consternation. They had never seen Rhodan like this before. Khrest almost cringed when Rhodan addressed him: 'You better retire to your quarters right away, Khrest. You too,

46

Thora. You'll be safest under the energy dome.'

'And you?' Khrest asked.

'I'll go with Marshall to direct the mutants. If anyone knows the answer to the impending questions, it'll be a mutant. Come on, Marshall. I've got a nagging feeling that we'll soon find out what our Mutant Corps is worth.'

As they went down in the elevator they could hear the alarm sirens wailing at the spaceport.

* * *

Bell was in his element, although he was firmly convinced that the alarm he conducted could be considered only a test. In case the Supermutant actually had succeeded in outwitting and capturing the *Good Hope*, he was unlikely to risk the valuable ship foolhardily, so Bell figured. On the other hand, he couldn't deny that Deringhouse behaved very peculiarly. He didn't respond to their calls but relentlessly and silently closed in on Terrania. He neglected to make the customary report and had broken off the search for the Supermutant prematurely without giving an explanation for his tactics.

All things considered, Bell concluded, there was ample reason to blow the alarm for Terrania.

Robot fighter units took up their positions around the extensive docks of the spaceport. Although the rayguns were inadequate against the defense screen of the *Good Hope*, Bell acted on instinct. The spaceport was located outside the protective energy dome and had to be prepared for all eventualities. Final decisions on defensive measures had to be made when their worst fears became reality. Bell still refused to reckon with that.

Meanwhile Rhodan briefed the Mutant Corps. He decided to refrain from deploying the new members and preferred to use only his experienced veterans. They all took the news in stride except Pucky who became quite excited.

The three-foot-tall mouse-beaver jumped restlessly up and down and hit the floor with his flat tail at every step. He furiously bared his incisor tooth and his reddish brown fur bristled. It would have been a mistake to regard the mouse-beaver as a normal 'animal' – he was much more than that. Rhodan had brought him back from a distant planet and assigned him to the Mutant Corps owing to his telekinetic abilities. Pucky was also a telepath and as such had easily learned the major languages of the Earth.

'That Supermutant!' he chirped in his high-pitched voice. 'This time I'm going to wipe him out! I couldn't get into the last fight.'

'Don't underestimate him,' Rhodan warned, stifling a smile. 'We don't know yet whether we'll actually be attacked. All we've now is a suspicion and we'll have to wait to see if it's confirmed. Marshall, try to get in touch with Deringhouse through the mutants who are suited for this special task. Take the tele-opticians and telepaths and let Marten make an attempt to get inside Deringhouse's mind and use his eyes. Time is of the essence. Pucky will accompany me to the spaceport. Betty Toufry, you'll have to come with me too. Marshall, you take over the command of the entire Mutant Corps and take the necessary actions. You'll receive the final go ahead signal as soon as the situation warrants. Is that clear?'

'Yes, sir!' the Australian acknowledged.

'We'll communicate by radio. Don't leave the protection of the energy dome under any circumstances unless you receive my special orders.'

He rushed out of the building with Betty Toufry and Pucky and got into a fast car that took him and his companions to the spaceport.

Rhodan had special reasons for selecting Pucky and Betty on this trip. Pucky's telekinetic powers were second to none. Sometimes he would steer an entire squadron of fast airplanes by remote control, no matter what the pilots did to resist. Betty Toufry on the other hand was a combination of telepath and telekinetic. She was only twelve years old but had the brain of a genius and talents to match. Rhodan secretly considered her the forerunner of the new human species which was in the process of development. She was way ahead of her time in every respect.

The alarm had caused the streets to appear deserted. It was already dusk and soon night would fall. Normally the night life of Terrania began at this hour but there was no sign of it tonight. The people on their way home from work had rushed into the nearest shelters, which still remained as mute witnesses of the turbulent times when the New Power first came into existence. The officials of the administration remained in their buildings or went down to the basement as required. The ride-walk conveyers kept rolling throughout the city but they were almost empty of people.

Only here and there a lone policeman made his rounds.

Rhodan left the city behind and raced along the thirty foot wide track toward the spaceport. The desert stretched to his left. Far away at the horizon it was already dark and in the west a glowing red sky blazed at the end of day.

Rhodan switched the steering of his car over to automatic radar and with his wristband transceiver contacted Colonel Freyt in the Central Command. 'Hello, Freyt! I'm on my way to the spaceport where Deringhouse will land – if he lands at all. Anything new? Did you make contact with the K-VII?'

'Nothing yet, sir,' Freyt replied. 'The *Good Hope* still refuses to answer. Perhaps their transmitter is defective.'

'That's a possibility,' Rhodan admitted but he remained skeptical. 'I think Deringhouse would have notified us about it via the Z-45 if such were the case. He knows perfectly well that we treat every spaceship that fails to identify itself before landing as hostile. Anyway, I'll keep my radio on reception. Let me know as soon as you hear of a change.'

Betty Toufry made big serious eyes. She looked from the side at Rhodan stroking Pucky's fur. 'Does it look that bad?' she asked as she read the anxiety in Rhodan's mind. 'What could happen?'

'Many things, Betty. We don't know yet and when we find out it may be too late. How far away can you receive mental vibrations, Betty? Do you think you can read Deringhouse's thoughts when he's still outside the Earth's atmosphere?'

'Could be. I'd require the precise direction for my concentration.'

'I'll see that you get it in time, Betty.'

Rhodan looked forward and switched off the automatic steering. The hangars emerged in the twilight. Only a few lights were burning and the landing field, usually bright as day, lay in almost total darkness in the desert.

Rhodan stopped in front of the main building. He hurried hand-in-hand with Betty to the entrance, followed by the waddling and cantankerous Pucky emitting shrill noises.

Bell breathed easier when he saw Rhodan enter. He was perched behind a gigantic control panel and operated at the same time the transceiver sets by which he directed the defense army as well as the movements of the robots. He issued a few more instructions, put some levers in neutral and leaned back. 'It's good to see you,' he said. 'I couldn't have managed much longer alone.'

'Is everything all right?' Rhodan wanted to know.

'As far as I can tell, yes. I'm beginning to believe that you're too pessimistic. Deringhouse will get a kick out of it when he sees the hullabaloo he's stirred up. Perhaps his transmitter has conked out ...'

'We don't have time to debate the pros and cons of our precautionary measures. Time is running out,' Rhodan told him.

At the same moment Rhodan's receiver began to buzz. It was Freyt.

'Are you all ready at the control tower?'

'Yes, you can switch over.'

A second later Freyt's face appeared on the video-screen. He stared vaguely for a moment into the room before he said: 'Deringhouse has slowed down his speed. The spacesphere has reached the Earth's atmosphere and is getting lower. If it follows its present direction it'll land on our territory.' He made a slight pause and then continued: 'We've got the K-VII on screen. No exterior damage or changes are visible. Coming closer. Defense screen not activated. I begin to believe we've been seeing ghosts.'

'I don't believe in ghosts,' Rhodan shot back and ended the conversation. Then he called Marshall. The telepath came on right away.

'Mutant Corps has started its operations, sir. Wuriu Sengu has already taken his first blurred look into the Command Center of the K-VII.' Sengu had the extra-ordinary gift of seeing through solid matter even at great distances. 'He claims Deringhouse is steering the spaceship. He's recognized Deringhouse in the pilot seat. Unusual, don't you think?'

'Why shouldn't the Commander conduct the ship himself during the landing?' Rhodan was baffled by Marshall's notion. 'Anything else?'

'Fellmer Lloyd received a weak brain-wave pattern which he couldn't identify. It was his impression that the pattern mainly reflected indifference. In addition he registered something very obscure and was unable to describe the feelings that moved the owner of the brain pattern.'

'Let him go on concentrating,' Rhodan ordered. 'Advise me immediately of any new developments.' Then he switched back to Freyt. 'Colonel, I require at once the exact position of the K-VII.'

Two minutes later Betty Toufry sat in a comfortable chair, closed her eyes and 'stared' at a slant toward the ceiling that presented no resistance to her probing thoughts. With bated breath Rhodan stood at her side waiting for the result. The face of the young girl suddenly took on a taut expression. She pressed her lips together and her hands trembled. She seemed to listen to a distant voice that she could barely understand. Then she opened her eyes. 'It's Deringhouse who's handling the controls – but then again it's not quite like Deringhouse. Some of the mutants we've captured earlier from the Supermutant displayed a similar thought pattern. I'm afraid ...'

Rhodan didn't lose a second. He called Freyt and instructed him to order alarm state #1. Marshall was also informed. Bell gave the army the necessary commands. The robots aimed their guns toward the sky which had in the meantime turned dark.

Terrania was ready for its reception of the Supermutant, who was approaching via the mind of Deringhouse.

Everybody knew that Deringhouse was doomed.

Lieutenant Carell of the Border Guard knew it too. His small unit was not equipped with ray-cannons that could have destroyed the Good Hope. It was his duty to guard the border of the New Power toward the east. He was just making the rounds for inspection and was in continual communication with the command post via a small transceiver. Since the border was not exposed to an acute danger, he patrolled the landing field and checked on the individual guards posted there.

There was the outline of a tremendous shadow against the dark horizon. It was *Stardust II*, the biggest spaceship in existence, half a mile in diameter, ultra-light-speed with armament that staggered the mind and a permanent crew of 500 men. Rhodan had wrested the ship away from the Topides when they attempted to conquer the Vega system.

Nearby stood the two heavy cruisers of the Terra class, *Terra* and *Solar System*, that had recently been built on Earth. Their diameter was only one-fourth of the *Stardust* and had the same spherical shape. The twelve Guppies of the same size as the other ships of the *Good Hope* class, ready to go, were farther in the background and waited for orders to take off.

Lieutenant Carell took notice of all the details while he listened to Rhodan's alarm orders. He was not certain that Deringhouse ...

This was Carell's last thought. As he was walking hale and hearty across the concrete landing field he became from one moment to the next an exploding atom bomb that melted the concrete within a large circumference. The bursting ball of fire illuminated the vast landing field as bright as day and made every detail clearly visible. A black mushroom cloud spread out and slowly rose up. Gradually the glowing flare faded away again.

The pressure- and heat-wave raced across the spaceport toward the ships lined up to start.

Rhodan and Bell observed the flash. The form of the explosion told them about the nature of the energy discharge. While the two men threw themselves to the floor to escape the shock-wave, Rhodan already called the fifteen spaceships: 'Take off at once! Keep in touch! Retreat to safe distance!'

Still sitting on the floor, Bell switched on the monitoring system of Terrania. Twenty optical screens lit up, showing the entire territory of the New Power from a bird's-eye view. The city stood out in relief under the observer. The lighted streets ran straight as arrows. To the side the desert stretched to the airport. The screens in the middle depicted the area under the energy dome where the vital centers of Rhodan's power were located.

With a stony face Bell watched as two robot-controlled ray-cannons situated at the edge of the landing field were incinerated in a blinding radioactive cloud. The incident was clearly visible in all its stages on the picture screen, rendering it the more mysterious. No shot had been fired at the installation and no bomb was thrown. *Good Hope VII* was too far away to hit it so accurately.

Nonetheless, atom bombs were exploding on the territory of the New Power!

'Impossible!' Bell groaned. Betty was still reclined in her chair. The shock-waves of the explosions had not yet ceased rumbling across the terrain. It was almost unbearably hot.

'There must be an explanation for this,' Rhodan muttered, realizing that he did not have one handy.

Several other spots on the screens began to blaze. Atom bombs coming from nowhere were detonated everywhere. Entire units of the robot army were blown up before they could go into action – against whom? Not even Rhodan was aware that the robots themselves had turned into atom bombs.

Colonel Freyt called urgently over the radio: 'Perry Rhodan! Emergency alarm! The K-VII is attacking us. It must be the K-VII under the command of Deringhouse. Khrest recommends the deployment of a gravitation bomb. He suspects that Deringhouse applies the new weapon of the Supermutant that enables him to initiate a fusion process with any matter over great distances. Awaiting your orders.'

A fearful quiet fell over the landing control tower.

Rhodan stared into Freyt's wide-open eyes. For the first time he could read in them absolute helplessness and he couldn't shake off a similar feeling himself.

'The G-Bomb,' he shuddered. 'On Earth? This could mean total ruin, Freyt. Tell Khrest that I dare not use the ultimate weapon. We must find another way out. For the time being you'll be safe under the energy dome.'

At the same moment Rhodan was made a liar. He clearly discerned from the corner of his eye how a fiery point appeared on the central screen, quickly grew and died away. The weapon of the Supermutant penetrated the defense shield of the Arkonides that had been impervious to the most destructive atomic rockets on Earth.

It was the end unless a miracle happened.

'Bell!' Rhodan's voice remained calm and collected. 'Take one of the three-man interceptors and get up into the stratosphere. Betty and Pucky will accompany you. Try to make contact with Deringhouse. Move!'

But Bell did not move. 'What about you?'

'Do what I tell you. Don't worry about me. I'll take the *Stardust* and follow with the other interceptors. Perhaps our hypnos will manage to break the will of the Supermutant.'

Bell rose slowly and looked at Betty. 'You want me to take a girl along? It's a matter of life and death.'

'I'm a full-fledged member of the Mutant Corps!' Betty protested indignantly. She knew no fear.

'Betty is our most potent telepath. If there's anyone who can ferret out the intentions of Deringhouse and the Supermutant, it's Betty. We'll keep in touch.'

At the same time Rhodan alerted the interceptors in the hangars. Freyt was notified. Marshall rushed with his mutants to the spaceport while two more robot fighters were atomized.

Bell, Betty and Pucky climbed aboard the Z-13, that was ready to go. The hatch was hardly closed behind them when the ship glided on the horizontal starting ramp out into the open and rose immediately at a steep angle up into the air. Then it shot with fantastic acceleration into the dark desert night-sky.

Down below to the left was suddenly a flaming hell, about where the small berth stood with the two interceptors held in reserve. Bell, who had looked inadvertently at the rear observation screen, was blinded and closed his eyes. He quickly figured out that neither Rhodan nor Marshall with his mutants could have already reached the interceptors.

Then he turned to the frontal observation panel. He switched on the night-vision sensor and in ten seconds got a clear picture of *Good Hope VII*. Deringhouse kept six miles above Terrania and had apparently no intention of landing.

'That must be him,' Pucky chirped in the back, catching his breath after the fast run. 'I don't see that he's throwing bombs.'

Bell didn't take his eyes off the screen as he slowed down the velocity of the Z-13. 'You can't see that because he's using a new weapon. Do you think you can get that buggy under telekinetic control?'

'Maybe.' Pucky doubted his capability. 'I'll try it.'

But he didn't get a chance to do it. *Good Hope VII* suddenly drew an elegant curve and soared with extreme acceleration out into space, leaving the Z-13 and the interceptors that had just become airborne, far behind.

Had the Supermutant called off his attack?

3   IVAN FOUR-EYES
(THE *OTHER* ULTIMATE WEAPON)

The first atom bomb of the Soviet Union was exploded in Siberia. It was an event that deeply surprised and frightened the western world. But it also alarmed the Soviet scientists themselves, at least some of those who were present at the explosion.

Ivan Vassiljevich Goratschin and his young wife Ludmilla were members of the experimental team and were caught in the radioactive fallout that was prematurely precipitated due to unfavorable climatic conditions. They were at once medically examined with the diagnosis that both of them must have received lethal doses.

Goratschin refused to be separated from his wife and to be sent to a hospital. He sensed deep in his heart that he had only a few months or a year at the most to live and had a premonition that he suffered a fate that would perhaps be shared in a few decades by whole generations.

He fled with his wife into the wilds of Siberia, covered all his tracks and disappeared. Somewhere near a river he joined some woodcutters who lived mainly from hunting and only reluctantly fulfilled their quota to the state. They asked no questions who the man and his pregnant wife seeking refuge were and gave them shelter. Later they helped him to build a hut and accepted gratefully his services as adviser for the local soviet. He was an expert at filling out the required forms for delivery to the government so that they had no more trouble with the inspection commissioners who visited the village every few years.

Ludmilla bore him a son.

The child was a monster with two heads weighing fifteen pounds at birth. He had a scaly skin and long sturdy legs.

It took all of Ivan's power of persuasion to prevent the villagers from killing his child. He invoked the right of the individual and the equality of men. The woodcutters relented but avoided close contact with the refugees who had settled among them.

The mutant grew up in the isolation of the village. When Ivan Ivanovich Goratschin was three years old everyone had become accustomed to his looks but his parents had died in the meantime.

Ivan Vassiljevich had quietly left one day and Ludmilla requested the woodcutters not to look for him. She knew that her husband wanted to spare the simple folks the sight of his misery. Soon she also felt that her time had come. The son with two heads was now three years old. He was already able to fend for himself and helped the woodcutters in the forest.

Thus Ludmilla disappeared one day too and never came back. Like her husband she died a lonely death in the woods.

At fifteen years Ivan was a full-fledged member of the community and nobody would have thought of teasing him because of his two heads. When strangers came Ivan went into hiding so that nobody found out about his existence.

When Ivan was twenty-three years old his self-confidence had grown so much that he decided to hide no longer when the next commission came to the village.

His sight first created a horrendous shock followed by amazement.

One of the visitors showed a special interest in Ivan. 'Wouldn't you like to come with me to the big city, my friend?' he asked him.

'No, I've no desire to leave,' he replied. Without another word he went with his friends down to the river to fish through holes in the ice.

Four months later the stranger came back, not alone this time. He brought along four soldiers in uniform carrying rifles. They claimed they came at the behest of the government and had orders to take Ivan with them.

The village did not dare draw the attention of the government. Ivan understood and respected their point of view. He was basically a very good-natured man and a double size Russian heart was beating in his eight-foot body. But this heart could also hate with doubled intensity when he was abused.

And now he had been cornered and his fury was aroused.

Ivan offered no resistance as the soldiers took him in their midst and led him away. The fur-clad stranger followed not too far behind. He kept both hands in his pockets and Ivan knew that he had his grip on his pistols.

The woodcutters gazed after the little group marching away and were reconciled never to see Ivan again. They really had learned to appreciate him. Hadn't he saved the lives of some who had become lost in the forest and had run out of matches? It had been bitter cold. The wood was frozen hard and they had no fire. But Ivan made a fire, a big blazing fire that kept burning brightly. He had simply stared at a spot and flames flared up. They warmed themselves quickly and gathered new strength, enabling them to find and return to their village.

Nobody had given much thought as to how Ivan had accomplished the feat of kindling a fire with the frozen wood.

It was long after dark when Ivan returned. His leg was bleeding; a bullet from the stranger had gone clean through. The woodcutters besieged him with questions but he refused to answer. He kept staring in the direction of the forest and the gentle slopes of the hills behind which lay the big tundra which had to be crossed in order to reach the cities of the people.

Then his eyes suddenly widened.

'They're coming back,' he muttered. The woodcutters shuddered and stared into the night but could see nothing except the dark trunks of the trees.

The men remained silent and followed Ivan's seeing eyes without finding the goal. The hill was almost six miles away and the night was pitch-dark.

Ivan closed his four eyes. He sat on a tree trunk, leaning slightly forward and supporting his body with his hands. For a second the light of a flashlight blinked. Now he knew where to concentrate his mental currents.

And then the incredible happened.

Behind the forest a brilliant explosion flared up, formed a glowing ball of fire and slowly rose up toward the invisible stars. When the light of the ball faded and became dark, a dimly lit cloud remained, looking like a giant mushroom. It spread out and took on eerie forms.

Soon a heat-wave engulfed the village, melted the last snow and tore wide cracks in the ice of the river that had already become thinner. The women screamed in terror and threw themselves on the ground. Ivan uttered an enormous laugh but the horror of what he had done began to creep into his laughter. Then men crossed themselves in awe.

They continued discussing the miracle for a long time but were unable to find an explanation. Ivan retreated to his hut and refused to see anyone.

Next morning at the crack of dawn they all went into the forest to the hilly slope. What they found there was even more astounding than the mysterious explosion the night before. A huge crater was gouged into the bare rock. The snow was molten and trees and bushes were uprooted. No living plants remained within a radius of one mile. The blackened area of devastation was almost round like a circle with the deep crater at its center.

Not a trace was left of the five kidnappers.

Therefore Ivan was considered to be Superman. He obviously relished his role and enjoyed giving little demonstrations of his uncanny powers. He was unaware that his gifts were the heritage of his unhappy parents whose genes had been changed so drastically by the lethal radiation dose.

Years later Clifford Monterny assembled his own Mutant Corps. Ivan would never have voluntarily followed the flabby stranger who appeared one day in the Siberian wilderness but Monterny was an irresistible hypno. He forced Ivan under his spell and compelled him to become his faithful servant.

Ivan had no choice but to obey and he followed Clifford Monterny to the United States where the headquarters of the Supermutant were located. There Ivan underwent his training that soon turned him into the most terrible weapon of destruction on Earth. Under the tutelage of the Supermutant, Ivan learned very fast to home in optically and mentally on targets over distances of many miles and to transform them into atomic energy.

Afterwards Monterny transported his most valuable mutant to Mars where he established a military base. The war against the New Power began.

It ended in Rhodan's victory but Monterny managed to escape and fled to Mars where he joined Ivan and two dozen other mutants he held under a permanent hypnoblock. Monterny often picked criminal elements as his helpers since their disappearance from the human society attracted far less attention than a missing solid citizen or public personality.

And now that Major Deringhouse in the *Good Hope VII* was on the verge of discovering the carefully kept secret of his support base on Mars, the Supermutant took action. Under no circumstances would he be willto pass up such a unique occasion to acquire possession of the spacesphere.

Everything went according to plan.

Deringhouse ordered his men to leave the ship. Seconds later they, too, were under the control of the Supermutant, who clamped his hypnoblock on them. The five remaining interceptors were temporarily secured in a ravine and the crew was imprisoned.

Major Deringhouse and twenty-five of his men were directed to launch a decisive attack on Perry Rhodan's headquarters in Terrania.

Ivan Ivanovich Goratschin was to serve as his most formidable weapon.

*   *   *

Major Deringhouse took his leave from the Supermutant toward whom he manifested neither friendly nor unfriendly feelings. He was so devoid of emotions that even the awesome sight of Ivan left him entirely cold.

Nevertheless, the mutants controlled by the Supermutant could not be described as perfect automatons. This was no longer the case, at least with Ivan, who had been able to regain a small part of his own thinking in the last three years. It was not enough to free him from the spell of his abominable master but it sufficed to make him ponder certain problems although they were at first of a secondary nature.

So he studied, for instance, the problem which of his two heads was the older and therefore had more authority.

The right head was called Ivan, although this was wrong and plainly nonsense. It claimed that it had become conscious three seconds earlier than the other one. This topic gave rise to hour-long disputes that always ended in futility since both heads possessed a common body and the same nervous system.

Just as erroneous as it was for the right head to be called Ivan, the left head was named Ivanovich. The Supermutant was responsible for this mistake since he disregarded the Russian custom that gave two names to each person. Ivan was Goratschin's proper first name whereas Ivanovich meant only 'son of Ivan.'

As it often happens, the error became a joke and stuck as lasting nicknames.

The *Good Hope* lifted off and Mars soon sank into the infinity of space. When Major Deringhouse passed the relay-station ship Z-45 he felt a vague sensation that he was supposed to do something but the voice of the Supermutant prevailed in his brain: 'Keep flying, Deringhouse. Don't pay attention to anything that happens outside your own vessel. Do you hear me? You don't have to worry about these details because I've already taken care of them. Continue on to Terrania without making reports. Stop at an altitude of six miles above the Terrania energy dome and do nothing.'

Deep down in his unconscious mind Deringhouse was relieved to receive the last command. He felt easier that he was not required to make use of his weapons albeit he was in no position to ignore such an order.

Finally the *Good Hope* hovered over Terrania. Complying with his orders all radio and range-finder sets were turned off so that Deringhouse failed to receive the urgent calls of Rhodan and Colonel Freyt.

He watched with apathy as the atomic blasts lit up the early night, believing that he and his men were not responsible for the holocaust. This assuaged the fears of his unconscious that were not completely eliminated.

Alone in his cabin Ivan Ivanovich sat on his bed and stared with expressionless eyes at the various picture screens. Time and again he emitted his concentrated fixations till he caught his first moving victim.

It was Lieutenant Carell.

Carell was a living organism, consisting partly of calcium and carbon atoms or their compounds. Ivan's mental vibrations through intensive concentration had the same effect on matter as a fuse on explosives. They released the energy of the matter instantaneously. Ivan could spontaneously turn a man into an exploding A-bomb.

However, he was not restricted to human beings. Carbon occurs in almost all combinations in the universe. Thus Ivan was not limited to his attacks on men but also detonated the robot fighters of the New Power. Indiscriminately he triggered the devastating atomic blasts on Earth without knowing the horrors he committed.

Meanwhile the Supermutant was safely on Mars and directed his 'detonator,' as he called the double mutant Ivan Ivanovich. This was his secret ultimate weapon with which he hoped to defeat Rhodan in the last battle.

The events were about to reach such a phase when something happened with which the Supermutant had failed to reckon. Ordinarily his hypnoblock was so firmly imposed that it could not be influenced or budged over great distances. But Rhodan had mutants too.

For instance, Betty Toufry.

Her first feeble contact with Deringhouse had resulted in nudging ever so slightly the hypnoblock of the strong willed but far distant Supermutant.

Or André Noir, the French hypno ...

Despite the fact that Noir's abilities were far less pronounced than those of the Supermutant, they were sufficient to sway a human being on board the *Good Hope*. Noir succeeded already during his headlong rush to the spaceport of Terrania in establishing regular contact with his 'victim,' partially counteracting the hypnoblock of the Supermutant.

At the same time Esper John Marshall caught frightening bits of thought. At first he didn't believe they could be human thoughts but then Fellmer Lloyd remembered having come across similar thought patterns during the first contact.

They doubtlessly came from the *Good Hope VII*.

And then the thought impulses ceased abruptly. The atomic explosions also came to an end. It did not even occur to Rhodan to suspect a connection between the two phenomena.

Simultaneously the *Good Hope* gathered fantastic speed and disappeared in the direction of Mars.

4 TWINHEAD IN TURMOIL

Bell was perplexed as he stared at the observation screen on which the spacephere shrank so rapidly that it looked like a ball falling into the abyss of eternity.

Pucky felt deprived of his chance to show what he could do. 'He's fleeing from me!' he consoled himself with a high-pitched whistling that expressed joy and anger together. 'He must have noticed that I wanted to grab him. The Supermutant is a coward!'

'Don't jump to such rash conclusions; they're usually wrong anyway,' Betty Toufry warned. She was lying in one of the big chairs. 'You're an excellent telekinetic but a lousy telepath ...'

'... and you're an excellent telepath but a lousy telekinetic!' Pucky countered furiously.

'You're absolutely right!' the girl agreed without getting upset. 'And that's why I know that you're wrong if you think the Supermutant is afraid of you.'

'Did you make contact with Deringhouse?' Bell broke in. He tried vainly to obtain a connection with Rhodan or Colonel Freyt.

'Not directly,' Betty shook her head. 'For a moment I thought I sensed his uncertainty but then his weak mental currents were superimposed by close and stronger ones.'

'The Supermutant,' Bell guessed without thinking.

Betty shook her head again. 'I said close! The

Supermutant is on Mars. He must have an effective agent on the *Good Hope* who is giving Deringhouse orders and whose thoughts I've intercepted.'

'And?' Bell inquired eagerly. He turned the knobs of the receiver till a constant hum became audible on the frequency of the New Power.

'He ordered Deringhouse to retreat immediately to the vicinity of the Moon.'

'Moon?' Bell reiterated, turning up the amplifier. 'How come the Moon?'

'I don't know,' the girl answered, seemingly at a loss. 'At any rate I didn't feel any trace of fear in the thoughts of the stranger, rather a sense of superiority and perhaps a little regret. I really don't understand this any longer.'

'Regret?' Bell glanced questioningly at Betty. 'Why would he order the destruction of the New Power and then feel remorse? Ah, there's Rhodan!' He adjusted the volume and switched on the picture. Rhodan's face appeared on the screen. His features reflected boundless amazement. Deep furrows in his face made him look years older.

'Hello, Bell! What's going on? We've lost Deringhouse.'

'What happened down there?' Bell wanted to know.

'Some localized damage but the bombardment suddenly ceased.' Rhodan obliged him first with the information, knowing that he couldn't get anything out of Bell before. 'The Mutant Corps and I are waiting in the interceptors. We're anxious to pursue Deringhouse but we lost sight of him.'

'He pulled back to the Moon,' Bell told him. 'Betty

has picked up some of their thoughts.'

'Very good. I'll proceed with the mutants to the *Stardust* and chase them. Freyt will follow me in his own space fighter ships. Keep on Deringhouse's track. Tell Betty not to lose contact with him.'

'Betty claims that somebody on board the *Good Hope* has caused the explosions on Earth and she thinks that he's now feeling some remorse,' Bell added hesitantly. 'He seems to be giving orders to Deringhouse.'

'Is that so?' Rhodan remained silent for a few seconds. 'I wouldn't mind if we could catch that man alive.'

'We're going to try,' Bell promised.

'Take up pursuit,' Rhodan finally said. 'We'll follow you at a safe distance. Keep your radio on reception.'

Bell manipulated his controls and before long got the *Good Hope VII* back on screen. The spacesphere had gone into orbit around the Moon.

Behind the Z-13 the Earth fell away like a stone in water. The metal sphere on the observation screen grew visibly. At the same time Bell kept listening to the exchange of information between Rhodan and the other ships. That way he kept up to date on the events behind him. Rhodan took over the *Stardust* and followed behind the Z-13 with moderate speed. Despite Deringhouse's dangerous behavior he seemed to have given up any intention of demolishing the *Good Hope VII*. Bell suspected that he was much too interested in the mysterious weapon to risk losing it by the total destruction of the spacesphere K-VII.

Ten minutes later Bell and his friends reached the

moon. He slipped into approximately the same path as the *Good Hope* and trailed the Guppy from a safe distance. Under the circumstances such assumptions had to be made with caution but he relied on Betty's assurances that no danger was imminent at the moment.

As soon as Rhodan affirmed that the *Stardust* was standing by for action, Bell made his next move. 'Pucky, you'll go ahead and disable the engines of the K-VII by teleportation. You know how to move the separator bebetween the two drive-sectors. Do you have enough telekinetic energy to do it? O.K., Betty, you keep in touch with Deringhouse and his guardian. You must warn us in case they plan an attack or some other detrimental action. Let's hope we'll be in luck. Let's go!'

He put his right hand on the trigger of the impulse-cannon and shifted with the left hand to medium acceleration, making the Z-13 race like a missile toward the distant *Good Hope*.

Pucky sat in a big upholstered chair and closed his eyes.

His great hour had come.

'Death to the Supermutant!' he chirped with his high voice and started to concentrate on the teleportation.

* * *

Ivan Ivanovich noticed that something began to bore into the brains of his two heads. Then he felt that a steel ring that had been tightened around both his foreheads was loosened.

Where was he?

Ivan's thought process started like a machine warming up. Long forgotten memories rose from the depth of his consciousness and began to round out the picture of his situation that was forming in him.

He shook both his heads, got up and walked over to the Command Center of the vessel. He had to duck at the door to keep from bumping his heads.

Major Deringhouse looked up as he saw the mutant enter. 'What's the matter, Ivan? Have you already taken care of everything?'

'What's there to take care of?' queried Ivan, shutting up his three-second-younger brotherhead Ivanovich. He sat down in an upholstered chair and studied Deringhouse attentively. Again he felt the boring probe in his brain but at the same time a different pressure emerged that had all the earmarks of dreadful hostility.

'Terrania, what else?' Deringhouse replied automatically without thinking. 'We had instructions to destroy Terrania.'

'What is Terrania?' Ivan wanted to know. 'Who gave us the order to demolish Terrania? And why?'

'I don't know why but I know ...' Deringhouse interrupted himself as the pressure in his brain grew almost painful. Then he heard a voice telling him distinctly: 'Come back, Major Deringhouse! Land on Mars at the same place you started from.'

The Supermutant had registered the changes taking place in his mutant Ivan and he realized after a futile attempt that he was unable to effect corrections across millions of miles. It also had become further apparent that his hypnoblock required renewal at certain intervals. It was his mistake that he had not found this out earlier.

'Return,' Deringhouse repeated the mental order of the hypno and grasped the controls. The *Good Hope* looped out into space and sped away with high acceleration.

Ivan listened inwardly as if he were hearing voices. Supermutant? Wasn't this the man who had abducted him three years before from the forest? The man he had obeyed ever since — was forced to obey! Why did he have to submit?

Gently and almost tenderly such thoughts pervaded his mind, reinforced by suggestion. They differed from those he had known for three years. They were free of threats and force, only persuasive and friendly. *Free yourself at last, Ivan,* they seemed to whisper. *Throw off the yoke of the Supermutant, Ivan, and begin to think for yourself!*

Think for myself, the mutant wondered and tried to understand what it could mean. Then he turned his attention to Major Deringhouse again, who sat immovably at the controls, steering the ship back to Mars.

The Supermutant was waiting for him on Mars. The closer they came to him, the worse the pressure in his head became again. He would be given new orders to start more and more fires ...

Slowly Ivan rose up and accosted Deringhouse. 'There's the Moon ahead of us. Don't go any farther!'

Deringhouse looked up with frightened eyes. 'But

the Supermutant ...'

'I'm giving the orders here, not the Supermutant,' Ivan stated sharply. He was suddenly overcome by a feeling that he must act or suffer the loss of something highly important. It was all rather vague and confused. He acted instinctively but consciously.

Major Deringhouse received the countermanding order of the Supermutant but failed to comply. The menacing giant standing beside him was a closer and much greater danger. Obediently he veered away from his course and let the *Good Hope* circle the Moon.

However the Supermutant was not yet ready to give up so easily. He pounded with strict orders the brains of the crew that had not yet been affected by the persuasion of Rhodan's mutants. It was impossible for André Noir to win each of the men with his hypnotic mental vibrations at the same time.

Ivan spun around when the door to the Command Center was pushed open and two men with drawn guns rushed in.

Ivan's fists shot forward. The left one was aimed by Ivanovich and the right by Ivan. The two men didn't know what hit them. The fists landed hard on their chins – and it was as if scales had suddenly dropped from their eyes. The burden on their brains was abruptly lifted. The dictates of the Supermutant ceased.

But they ceased only because Noir began to subject the wretched victims to his own treatment.

Yet there were twenty-three other men on board who would have given their lives for the Supermutant had he demanded it.

Ivan leaped forward, caught the crumpling assailants and put them gently on the hard metallic floor. Then he barred the door to the corridor with the magnetic lock that could not be opened from the outside. Only ten seconds later the first blows battered against the door.

Deringhouse remained undecided.

Again he heard distinctly the luring voice inside him that was evidently bolstered by a psychobeamer without which he would have been prevented from receiving it.

'Deringhouse, are you listening? Ignore the demands of the Supermutant. Do you understand me? This is Betty Toufry speaking. You remember me, don't you? We're near you. Don't do anything. Let the ship drift. Answer me in your thoughts if you've got my message. I can understand you.'

Concurrently another even stronger voice insisted: 'I'm the only one you must obey, Deringhouse. Get into high gear and return to Mars at once. Don't listen to anybody else. Have your men lock up Ivan. Do as I tell you!'

Deringhouse put his hand on the accelerator lever. Ivan did not let him out of his sight.

Deringhouse hesitated. The soft voice was back, this time more urgent and closer. 'Listen to Betty, Deringhouse! Do you want to betray me and Perry Rhodan? The Supermutant is our enemy. He's going to kill you if you go back to Mars. Wait for us and don't listen to the Supermutant!'

Ivan watched Deringhouse pull his hand slowly and reluctantly back from the lever.

'We want to wait,' Deringhouse said quietly but not without emphasis. 'Switch on the observation screens so we can take a look around.'

Stars sprang out from the black infinity and filled the screens. Close by was a round shadow that was lengthened and gleamed like silver as the light of the nearby Moon fell on it. Deringhouse remembered darkly that he had ships just like that in the hangar of the *Good Hope*, or did at one time. His brain was beginning to function again and told him that the ship could therefore not be hostile.

The Supermutant on Mars perceived that he was beginning to lose his control over Deringhouse. He tried it again with Ivan. 'Set fire to your pursuers, Ivan! They are out to kill you and me – me to whom you owe everything. Act without delay and execute my commands! Remove Deringhouse!'

Ivan slowly shook both his heads and said loudly so that Deringhouse could hear it too: 'No, Supermutant, I won't listen to you and I'm not going to kill Deringhouse. I want to wait because I've become curious and I would like to know what the others have done to me that I have to exterminate them.'

No reply came from distant Mars.

Deringhouse and Ivan gazed impassively at the observation screen and let the spacesphere continue girdling the Moon. The interceptor closed in on them. Farther away the magnification of the image sensors showed more ships, among them a gigantic spacesphere of incredible dimensions. They kept at a safe distance and Ivan began to suspect the reasons for it.

But why did the single interceptor dare come so close?

He was to find out sooner than he expected.

*　　　*　　　*

Bell knew only too well that the energy screen of the Z-13 was utterly inadequate to protect him against the uncanny weapon of the Supermutant. He had already learned that the effective range of the weapon was six miles. When he approached this limit and passed into the danger zone he was aware of the risk he took.

However he was willing to trust Betty. 'Have you already established contact with Deringhouse?' he asked as he raced straight to his goal. He flicked a glance at Pucky: 'Did you pull it off already?'

'They have no more energy left except their emergency reserve batteries,' the mouse-beaver whispered. 'Shall I give them a tumble?'

'Wait a little,' Bell pleaded. 'What's the matter, Betty?'

'Noir has gained partial control of the Supermutant's agent. The Supermutant keeps telling him to immolate us but I don't know what he means by that.'

'Immolate?' Bell murmured as his eyes suddenly narrowed. He was thinking about the atomic blasts in Terrania. 'And this agent refuses to do it?'

'Noir has managed to throw him into confusion. He now resists doing it.'

'Excellent! What about Deringhouse?'

'I believe he's listening to me,' Betty replied. 'What

78

are you going to do now?'

However Bell did not have a ready answer for that. He turned to Pucky instead: 'Can you disable the whole crew of the ship without anybody getting hurt?'

Pucky got up on his hindfeet, supporting himself with his wide beavertail. He folded his frontpaws over his chest and began to concentrate. In the meantime Bell communicated on the videoscreen with Rhodan who had followed him at a great distance with the mutants in the *Stardust II*.

There wasn't much time for conversation.

'Noir has asserted his influence on a certain Ivan,' Rhodan reported quickly. 'But we can't tell how long this will last.'

'Pucky has already gone into action,' Bell encouraged proudly. 'The K-VII has lost its thrust and they're out of energy.'

'Sounds familiar,' Rhodan replied.

'But it works,' Bell was quick to answer. 'And now Pucky is about to render the crew harmless. It's getting time for our mutants to intervene. That's where the teleporters come in.'

'Kakuta and Ras Tschubai are already waiting for the signal to go ahead,' Rhodan said tersely. 'When can I expect it?'

Bell noticed a nod from Pucky who was deeply absorbed in his endeavor.

'Just keep tuned in and you'll know when you can send your spacejumper's on their trip.'

Rhodan scowled. 'You mean the teleporters?'

Bell gave no answer and Betty spoke up: 'I've got the impression that Deringhouse will remain inactive for the time being. But Ivan seems to have rid himself entirely of the Supermutant's dominance. As far as I can make out the mixed-up thoughts, he must have knocked out two men of the crew when they wanted to force Deringhouse to fly to Mars.'

Pucky, who had left in the meantime, now triumphantly announced via the micro-telecom: 'They're all stuck to the walls of the cabins and can't move, but I can't keep it up much longer.'

'Perry!' Bell shouted at the top of his voice. 'You can dispatch Kakuta and Ras right now. We're ready. As soon as you give me the word I'll move in and get into their ship.'

'If you take my advice, leave well enough alone. I'll attend to it myself. Let Pucky watch out that there will be no mishaps. As long as Deringhouse and his men can't move a muscle we'll be safe from that confounded weapon.'

Bell cursed under his breath. Once again he had to do the hazardous preparatory work and now when it got interesting he was supposed to stand by as a spectator while others finished the operation. There had to be a fly in the ointment. He ...

He was unable to finish his train of thought. Pucky came back, flaunted his tooth, smoothed his bristling fur in the nape of his neck and settled down to relax. 'I think the two teleporters can take care of the rest,' he chirped. He was apparently not in the least disappointed that others finished the job he had started.

'Bell, I've pressed the men gently against the walls and I'm holding them there. This requires only half the effort of concentration but I can't sit here forever.

The point is to liberate the men from the spell of the Supermutant.'

Bell glanced at the observation screen. 'Here he comes!' he exclaimed.

The gigantic *Stardust* swooped down and joined the *Good Hope* and the Z-13 on their path around the Moon, followed by the other interceptors. Then the big battleship pulled abreast of the *Good Hope* and a panel in the gleaming silvery hull slid back exposing an oval opening – the access hatch to the huge hangar that could hold twelve ships the size of the *Good Hope*. Bell saw the flash of a tractor-beam and watched as the captured ship, together with Deringhouse, Ivan and twenty-five men, was hauled into the gaping mouth of the voluminous sphere.

Bell sighed contentedly. He looked at Betty and asked: 'Well, little girl, what is Deringhouse thinking now?'

The girl stroked her forehead: 'It's a complete suspension of thought, to describe it properly. I can't detect a thing.'

Bell grinned and stared at the observation screen showing the *Stardust II*. 'I'd love to know what's going on in that mothball.'

Rhodan smiled down from the screen. 'Come over Bell. Down the hatch! Hurry up!'

Ten seconds later the Z-13 entered the hatch that had been kept open and touched down next to the immobilized *Good Hope*.

Pucky suddenly stopped smiling. He nodded to Betty from the telecom screen. Being also a telepath he had understood what was going on in her mind. 'I won't let him go,' he chirped.

'Who?' Bell wanted to know.

'Please don't disturb Pucky now,' Betty said with unaccustomed seriousness. 'I've intercepted some very evil thoughts that are bent on our destruction. Ivan is thinking about setting another fire.'

Bell, who had already risen from his chair, fell back. He felt paralyzed. He expected any moment to become an exploding atom bomb that would blow his ship and the *Stardust* to ... stardust.

*　　*　　*

Ivan Ivanovich Goratschin was cognizant of the fact that he had broken the spell that had ruled his existence for three years. He surmised that he had fallen victim to a criminal.

The thoughts of the Supermutant were demanding and vicious; the new ones that tantalized his brain were full of friendliness and goodwill. Of course this could be a deception. But now he had regained his faculties and wanted to decide for himself which side was in the right.

When Pucky intervened, the light and the ventilation were the first to be interrupted. Deringhouse determined at once that the energy reactor was exhausted. The emergency batteries quickly restored the illumination but the air circulation was blocked and it became stuffy and cold in the Command Center.

A few seconds later Ivan felt himself lifted up by an invisible force and irresistibly pressed against the wall. He was completely helpless with his two heads pushed against the cold circular window hatch. He was able to look out but he saw nothing except empty space. The intruders came from the opposite side.

His first reaction was one of wrath against those who tried to render him helpless. Did they know his secret? If so, they deliberately took a terrible risk. At this moment Ivan was ready to turn anybody who would venture into his view at the window into a bursting bomb. However he didn't see a soul; not even the mouse-beaver entered into his line of sight.

The soothing thoughts again pervaded his two brains. 'Don't be afraid, Ivan, we want to help you. But we have to be careful so you won't hurt us. We desire peace with you and your men.'

And a little later: 'We're going to pull you into our ship.'

Although Ivan was unable to look to the side, he saw from the corner of his eye that Deringhouse was stretched out on the console unable to lift his head an inch.

Soon the void was replaced by the sight of a brightly lit hall in which some people ran around excitedly.

Ivan still harbored ideas of annihilation. He could clearly see the people and it would have been easy for him to atomize them and blow up the ship into which he had been hauled. However two things prevented him from carrying out his intentions.

By now he had learned to gauge the effect of his formidable gift and he knew that he would kill himself too if he detonated a man in the hall. Furthermore, he was enticed by the strange thoughts his brain received. The tender voice exerted such an attractive influence on him that it created the wish to meet the owner. Yet if he were to set another fire, his spiritual partner would also be doomed.

And finally there was a third reason added. A new voice spoke to him, cold and urgent, but entirely different from the Supermutant. 'You must stop hurting people, Ivan! You're among friends who are anxious to help you. You must never again misuse your great gift for destructive ends. Henceforth it should be used for the good of mankind.'

Ivan hesitated for a second but he knew that he would voluntarily bow to the pleading, making up his own mind. Exercising his own free will was a radically new experience for him and it gave him great pleasure.

Deringhouse by contrast felt extremely unhappy. His brain was also exposed to the calming thoughts and he felt their well-meaning effect but he was still under the influence of the Supermutant's hypnoblock. The order to return to Mars was passed through nerves to his hands but his hands were unable to move. They were pressed against the controls, condemned to paralysis like his whole body. A mysterious power held him in its grip.

And the twenty-five men of the crew shared the same fate.

Deringhouse and Ivan heard that the hatch was opened although it was impossible to reach the lock from the outside – not even considering the fact that the *Good Hope* had been deprived of all energy. Only vaguely did Deringhouse recollect that such incredible feats could be performed by the mental emanations of mutants.

André Noir took care of Deringhouse as soon as they entered the Command Center. Not even the terrible sight of the two-headed monster could keep him away. The two teleporters emerged in the quarters of the crew and began to tie up the incapacitated men. This was for the moment the only possible thing to do since Rhodan's mutant corps had only one hypno available with the ability to break the spell of the Supermutant.

Meanwhile Bell and Betty Toufry climbed out of their interceptor and caught up with Rhodan in the hangar of the *Stardust II*.

'Good job,' Rhodan quickly congratulated.

'H'm,' Bell muttered enviously. 'Betty has contributed a lot to make our task successful.'

'I haven't forgotten that,' Rhodan smiled, patting the little girl on the head. 'Are you still in contact with Deringhouse?'

'No.' Betty shook her head, to his surprise. 'Noir has taken over. But I'm maintaining contact with Ivan. He's a very odd person. I can't quite figure him out. In any case he's the one who manipulates the uncanny weapon. His hypnoblock has been completely lifted. The Supermutant lost all his influence over him.'

'Oh, we've got it made,' Bell sighed with relief.

'Not quite,' Betty disappointed him.

Rhodan listened attentively. 'Why not?' he asked.

'I can read in his thoughts that he's still capable of obliterating us. Even his state of paralysis couldn't prevent him from doing it.'

'And why doesn't he do it?'

Betty blushed. 'He's curious — curious to see me.'

Rhodan exchanged a quick warning glance with Bell.

'So he's curious to see you? In that case we should fulfill his wish. The sooner, the better. Let's go to the Z-VII and have a look at Ivan.'

They let the mutants go in first before they entered the airlock of the Z-VII themselves.

Betty was growing more nervous. She received Noir's confused thoughts and surmised that they concerned Ivan. She rushed so much that Rhodan and Bell had trouble following her.

Betty arrived before they did. She stood beside André Noir and stared at a giant with two heads who returned her gaze with undisguised astonishment in his four eyes.

Each of the partners comparing their thoughts had imagined an entirely different mental picture.

Betty was seized by a shock and a terrible fear. She had expected to find a man or perhaps a mutant but not an ogre with two heads.

And Ivan? From the first moment that he heard the telepathic voice with the sympathetic undertone, he had been filled with the desire to know the owner. And now a little slip of a girl was facing him.

Rhodan came in, followed by Bell and Pucky. He realized at once the precarious situation. He saw the young girl's shock and instinctively felt the peril that could develop if the monster realized the truth. Only because Ivan had felt sympathy for Betty had he become disinclined to trigger further blasts.

He nodded to the monster with a perfectly restrained face. 'You're Ivan, I presume. My name is

Perry Rhodan and I've come to negotiate with you.'

Not a word about what had happened previously and no remark that he had succeeded in capturing Deringhouse and Ivan. Not the slightest sign that he was horrified by his freakish sight, only a friendly approach in an atmosphere of equality.

Ivan's attention was distracted from Betty. 'I'm Ivan Ivanovich Goratschin,' the two heads nodded in unison 'My master is ... was ... Clifford Monterny, the Supermutant. I've come to the conclusion that I've committed many wrongs.'

'It wasn't your fault, Ivan. You've used your weapon against people you didn't know because you were under the control of a powerful man who got off on the wrong track. I emphasize again, Ivan, that you were not to blame and that nobody is going to hold you responsible. Only the Supermutant is guilty and we'll see to it that justice will be done.'

'I'm willing to help you,' Ivan volunteered, glancing questionably at Betty. 'I'll do anything in my power if you're not affronted by my unusual appearance.'

'Look at Pucky,' Rhodan told him, making room for the mouse-beaver to come out of his hiding place. 'Nobody can honestly say that he looks like a normal person but we all love him dearly.'

'He's not a human being,' Ivan murmured bitterly, 'but I'm supposed to be one.'

'It's only the quality of character that makes a difference,' Rhodan stressed. 'When it comes to cosmic thinking, variations of race and appearances have ceased to be of importance. The Supermutant looks human but he's in truth an abominable fiend. But you, Ivan, probably have more human feelings than people showing a smooth facade and who knowing how to talk smoothly.'

Two faces glanced sideways at Betty who had long before understood what Rhodan had in mind for her. She gulped bravely and forced herself to smile. Then she stretched her little hand out to Ivan. 'We were friends from the start and we want to remain friends in the future. If you like, you may call me Betty.'

The face of the mutant shone with a happy smile that moved Rhodan deeply. He realized how miserable this unfortunate being must have been in the past — rejected by men and abused by the Supermutant. Now, perhaps for the first time in his life, he encountered respect and true friendship.

Ivan took hold of Betty's outstretched hand reverently, then squeezed it carefully, suggesting a bow, and replied: 'Thank you, Betty. I'll never forget that we're friends although ...' He hesitated for a second, looking disconcerted. Then he continued with fortitude: 'Although I happen to look different.'

Perry had been afraid that Betty might have trouble concealing her surprise. However all members of the Mutant Corps had been thoroughly impressed with the concept that a living being should never be judged by appearance and that only attitudes and capabilities counted.

Pucky could no longer restrain himself. He squeezed himself past Betty, stood up on his hindlegs and extended both paws toward the startled Ivan. 'I wish to be your friend as well. Don't hold it against me that I hung you up on the wall. I did it only to keep you from blowing us to bits.'

Ivan took the paws, pressed them gently and said: 'I could have destroyed you all regardless. I could do it even now without moving from this spot.'

These words of the twinhead reminded Rhodan of his most vital problem. 'It would interest me to know exactly what the Supermutant has in his arsenal,' he said, turning to Ivan. 'It might become necessary to turn his weapon against him if he uses it to attack us again.'

For a moment Ivan seemed confused but then he understood. A knowing smile mixed with pride crossed his two faces. 'Fear no more, Perry Rhodan! The Supermutant has lost his weapon. He will never again deploy it against you.'

Rhodan failed to comprehend the meaning of his words. Betty, who was probing the thoughts of the mutant, suddenly blanched. Rhodan noticed and became worried. What was going on here? He tried to look Ivan in the eyes, not knowing whether to choose his left or right head. The mutant didn't make it easier for him but challenged him with his right head: 'Why can't he use this weapon against us? Because *I am* this weapon. I can transform any matter containing calcium or carbon into energy. All I have to do is detonate it.'

'How?' Rhodan asked. He, too, had turned a little pale as hundreds of possibilities flashed before his inner eyes of how this sport of nature could with one thought obliterate him and the whole Earth. Bell stood stockstill.

'I don't know,' Ivan admitted. 'Do you know how you can see or smell? You can hear but you don't know why or how you hear. You simply do it, instinctively and without special effort. Perhaps science will some day find an explanation for my feat. I can look with my eyes at an object and if I concentrate on it, it becomes an atom bomb.'

Rhodan regained his composure. 'You realize that, in a sense, you have become a successor to the Supermutant. Up to now Clifford Monterny was considered to be the most dangerous man in the Solar system. Henceforth it'll be you, Ivan, and your conscience will have to decide whether your gift will be a benefit for the good or whether it will serve evil purposes.'

Ivan smiled and looked at André Noir, who just had returned to the Command Center. 'Haven't I already decided this? Would you all be still alive if I had chosen with an evil mind? I'll always be on the side to which Betty belongs. I owe it to her first tender thoughts that the ring about my head was broken. How can I ever forget what she has done for me?'

Betty agreed eagerly: 'I know that your innermost thoughts match your words, Ivan. I'll always care for you both and when I say Ivan I also mean Ivanovich.'

Rhodan felt vast relief, not only because he knew that from now on Ivan would be on his side but mainly also because he could assume that the Supermutant, shorn of his atomic bomb trigger, was relatively harmless.

'I'd be grateful to you, Ivan, if you and the Mutant Corps would seek each other's friendship. Men like you are desperately needed to shape the history of mankind. And now we want to join together in the pursuit of our mutual enemy.'

'Yes, sir!' Pucky chirped cheerily and suddenly floated up to the height of Ivan's faces. 'Death to the Supermutant! Justice will prevail!'

André Noir came closer and shoved the mouse-beaver to the side. He offered his hand to Ivan. 'Welcome to our midst, Ivan. I'm convinced that you've finally shaken off the hypnoblock of the Supermutant. Now you're one of us.'

'Thank you!' Ivan answered, deeply touched. And 'Thank you' added Ivanovich, who had remained silent throughout.

Twinhead was at peace with themself.

5   FLIGHT OF THE SUPERMUTANT

The relay station ship Z-45 circled for weeks around Mars at a constant distance of nine million miles. It carried only a crew of two men, the commander Lieutenant Bings and the radio-technician Sergeant Adolf. The two men had been close friends for many years. They had studied together at the Space Academy and passed their exams. Susequently they were selected by Rhodan for his fleet.

Bings had a hobby: a passion for collecting butterflies. Nothing peculiar in itself but a little unusual for a spaceman. Unfortunately his friend Adolf also had a hobby: he too collected butterflies! This always provoked bitter fights that usually ended with Sergeant Adolf losing a rare specimen of his collection to Bings. Each of the men guarded his treasures like the apple of his eye and whenever one of them was able to add a new butterfly to his collection, he made the other man's mouth water till he was shown the magnificent specimen. That of course only increased his appetite.

'I'm not really that keen on your Venusian Palpitating Eye butterfly,' Bings said, glancing at the observation screen with a bored look, 'but it's not yet in my collection. Sooner or later I'm sure to get one but at the moment I could use it.'

'At the moment you can't have it anyway.' Adolf referred to the facts of their situation. 'But suppose I would give it to you later, what could you offer me in exchange?'

'How would you like to have my Black and White Transmuter that you've always admired so much? You know it's the only specimen in existence.'

'Yes, you never fail to mention that,' Sergeant Adolf muttered sullenly. 'But I like my Palpitating Eye better.'

'It's not really worth that much,' Bings tried to tell him with an indifferent expression as if he were bored by the conversation. 'I can always find one on Venus or ask somebody to get me one.'

'Why don't you try it,' Adolf proposed and fell silent, feeling offended. The Palpitating Eye was his pride and joy, especially because his friend Bings lacked it.

Lieutenant Bings was about to renew the praises of his Black and White Transmuter when he stared at the observation screen with tightened lips. Exactly in the center was a tiny blip that slowly wandered off to the right. He turned hastily to Adolf: 'Magnification! Quick! What kind of ship is that? It's too small for a Guppy.'

'Maybe it's a Black and White Transmuter,' the Sergeant murmured disrespectfully, getting to work at his instruments. The shifting point was on the verge of leaving the right edge of the screen. Adolf adjusted the magnification and focused on the segment containing the point till it became clear. Reddish shining Mars moved to the left.

The ship, if it was one indeed, came from Mars.

'An interceptor,' Lieutenant Bings whispered. 'I

wonder if it's one of ours.'

'The Supermutant has also acquired some interceptors,' Adolf pointed out. 'It's just as likely that it could be him. Ever since the Z-VII silently sailed past us, I believe that anything is possible.'

From their present position Mars was sandwiched between them and Earth. Therefore it was also possible that a ship approaching from Earth appeared deceptively to come from Mars. The commander of the Z-45 took this posibility into account, if for no other reason simply so as not to concede that his Sergeant was right. 'Nonsense! The Supermutant is not about to venture out, running risks. He'll sit on Mars till doomsday if we don't make it hot as hell for him.'

'There're supposed to be some weird bugs in the sands of the Martian deserts ...'

'You better watch out and don't neglect your duty,' Bings warned angrily and stared at the observation screen where the gliding point was followed by the tele-lens with equal speed. 'The ship is proceeding in a direction that must lead it to Jupiter,' he stated incredulously. 'Who can understand this?'

'Who wants to?' Adolf asked without expecting an answer. More out of boredom than from a sense of duty he began to check the other screens and suddenly exclaimed with surprise, 'What do you know? Look at that traffic jam! Soon we'll have the same traffic problem up here as on Earth where they've already started to park their cars up in the air in anti-grav fields.'

'What do you mean?' Bings inquired.

'There comes another ship,' was the reply.

Bings sat up and visibly wavered in his decision as to which one of the two ships to observe. Fortunately he was automatically relieved of the burden of choice when Sergeant Adolf pushed a button causing both screens to follow their objectives.

The second ship approached on a virtually direct course. The reason it was not absolutely straight stemmed from the fact that the course had to lead around Mars. As they soon determined it was also an interceptor. When the ship finally came within a few miles they could clearly read the name on its side: Z-13.

'Thirteen, of all things!' Sergeant Adolf was exasperated. 'I'm not exactly superstitious but ...'

'Better pay attention to your job!' Bings admonished his comrade. 'Is this one of the ships that have been reported stolen?'

It was not on the list and so they waited with their eyes glued to the receiver. Soon the communication screen began to light up and a broad round face with pale eyes and a grinning mouth appeared on it.

'It's us,' Bell said and added: 'Anything new?'

'Nothing exceptional,' Bings reported dutifully, then remembered the ship moving in the direction of Jupiter. 'Actually there was something. We've observed an interceptor on outward bound course.'

'Outward bound' means – in the language of the astronauts – away from the Solar System from their respective position.

Bell nodded to somebody who was next to him and said: 'We'll be over in a minute. Prepare the vacuum gangway.'

Sergeant Adolf muttered disgustedly: 'I knew it, that blasted thirteen ...'

*　　*　　*

'It's not our job to eliminate the Supermutant,' Bell reiterated once more. Sergeant Adolf's face showed little enthusiasm. 'Tatjana has succeeded in detecting from a great distance some very unusual activities on Mars. With her natural defense mechanism she can conduct a telepathic surveillance of the Supermutant without any risk whatsoever of him forcing her under his hypnotic spell. With our special helmets we're insulated from his influence to a degree. As I told you, all we're required to do is check up on what happened on Mars. Your observation confirms our conjectures. The Supermutant has fled in an interceptor after learning of his defeat on Earth. What are we going to do about it? Pursue him or return to Earth?'

'Death to the Supermutant!' Pucky's shrill voice came from the corner. He sat there on his tail, munching happily on a fresh carrot Lieutenant Bings had got him from the refrigerator. 'We'll chase him and clobber him! It's the only thing to do.'

'You keep your mouth shut!' Bell shouted exasperatedly, holding on to a brace in case Pucky resented being browbeaten and took some vengeful action. 'We're supposed to gather information, nothing else. Rhodan wants to double-check on Ivan before he lets him loose against the Supermutant.'

'We don't need Ivan,' Pucky grumbled impatiently. 'I can take care of him.'

'But it's against our orders,' Bell admonished, and

96

turned to Bings and Adolf. 'We're supposed to find out what's going on on Mars. I've already said that Tatjana ...'

'Do you believe that the interceptor we've discovered had some connection with the Supermutant?' Sergeant Adolf asked.

Bell looked questioningly at Tatjana Michalowna, the telepathic girl who at one time had also lived under the control of Monterny and had been rescued by Rhodan.

'I can receive his thoughts, they're full of panic and wrath. The Supermutant already sees Mars as a glimmering red star which means that he's out in space. Yes, Sergeant, I do believe that he's getting away on board that interceptor.'

'What are we waiting for?' Pucky shouted indignantly. His high-pitched voice was so loud that Bell was afraid it would burst his eardrums. Nevertheless he ignored his objections and told Lieutenant Bings: 'Call Rhodan! Hurry up!'

Bings' face looked confused, giving Sergeant Adolf secret satisfaction and joy. 'Do you want me to violate the radio silence, sir? Only in an emergency ...'

'This *is* an emergency!' Bell bellowed. 'How much longer do I have to wait?'

Tatjana Michalowna shook her head imperceptibly. It was the first time she had seen Bell so excited. There was not the slightest reason to be so incensed. Could it be that he was afraid to wage a headon fight against the Supermutant? Or was he really so meticulous about adhering to his directions. She listened for a moment to his thoughts and then smiled knowingly.

Lieutenant Bings beckoned to his Sergeant. Adolf switched on the telecom set and in a few seconds got his colleague from the *Stardust II* on the screen.

'Urgent call to Perry Rhodan. Personal!'

'Just a minute.' Soon Rhodan's face appeared on the screen. 'Yes. Z-45?'

'Lieutenant Bings, sir.' Bings pushed his Sergeant aside. 'Mr. Reginald Bell wishes to talk with you, sir.'

Bell, in turn, eased Bings out of the way.

'The Supermutant has left Mars and is fleeing in the direction of Jupiter. Shall I pursue him? He's got only one interceptor.'

'I'm not sure that I should call on Ivan yet for help. It would be better if I follow you with the mutants in the Guppy.'

'That won't be necessary, Perry,' Bell assured him. 'We can handle him ourselves. Tatjana has already latched onto him and we can track him down.'

Rhodan thought for a moment and then assented: 'Very well. Take up the pursuit but be careful. I won't be able to follow you that soon since Ivan still requires the attention of Betty and myself. I don't dare leave him alone without supervision. Good luck! Anyway, you're two interceptors against one.'

The telecom screen went dark again.

Sergeant Adolf stood flabbergasted in the corner and looked reproachfully at Bings. 'Thirteen!' he murmured disconsolately. 'I knew it all the time.'

Lieutenant Bings ignored his friend and turned to Bell. 'Sir, don't you frequently go to Venus? I wonder if you could occasionally bring me a Palpitating Eye butterfly?'

Bell looked so dumbfounded that Pucky squealed with laughter and practically rolled on the floor. He smacked against the metal plates with his broad tail and squeaked: 'Palpitating Eye! He wants a Palpitating Eye butterfly! Any other wishes, Lieutenant?'

Bings seemed to feel insulted. He made no reply.

Bell said rather helplessly: 'Perhaps they can be found on Jupiter, too ...'

6 'MONTERNY MUST BE FOUND!'

Clifford Monterny could feel that his telepath link with the mutant Ivan was getting weaker and weaker. In his desperation he gave Ivan one last command to detonate everything in sight but was frustrated by a strong hypno counterblock that intervened between him and Ivan and isolated his brain.

The Supermutant finally realized that he had lost his most effective weapon and with it the last round. Rhodan and his mutants had proved to be too mighty for him.

Give up?

He slowly shook his head and surveyed the installations he had built during the last year under the surface of Mars. Most of the equipment had been salvaged from an interceptor, even the generator including the mini-reactors. The ship was no longer fit for action.

If he decided to escape he could use only one of the interceptors and take only two of the remaining twenty-five men with him. The other twenty-three had to be left behind.

And where could he flee?

The only place where it was relatively safe for him was somewhere in the empty space beyond Mars. He had to try to find there a temporary abode till they forgot about him on Earth. Then he could one day return perhaps and ...

The thought of revenge restored his energy.

He rose up abruptly and turned off the observation screens, severing his contact with the outside world.

He took one last look at his hide-out and went out to the corridor. He stopped at another door, hesitated for a moment and opened it. A few men stared at him curiously.

Their eyes began to light up. Perhaps he came to tell them that the time of their exile had come to an end?

Clifford Monterny was able to read their thoughts and decided to play along. It would be the best way to keep the existing hypnoblock in force with the least possible strain.

'After a few more preparations have been made the period of inactivity on Mars will be concluded,' he said in a firm voice. 'For this purpose it is necessary that I undertake a reconnaissance flight. You stay here and wait till I come back. If any strangers attempt to invade the fortress, you must prevent them at all costs. Wallers and Raggs, you'll accompany me. We'll take the Z-35 to scout.'

Two men rose up. One of them put his jacket on as if he were going on a short walk. Both took their oxygen masks. The hangar with the intact and the ransacked interceptor was also located beneath the surface and was connected by a walkway with the center itself, but it was outside the air supply system.

The Supermutant carefully closed the door and went with the two men to the storage room. He put on a fur jacket and took a mask as well. For a moment he considered the five captured interceptors and their fifteen man crew in the uniform of the New Power. But then he shrugged his shoulders. Even if he manned the five ships with his own people it wouldn't mean more security for him. The risk of being detected was so much smaller for a single ship. Six interceptors certainly had more fire-power but Monterny had an inkling that this wouldn't matter very much any more in the long run.

And so it happened that the fifteen officers and men of the five captured interceptors that belonged to the *Good Hope VII* and were held ready to start in a ravine near the plateau, sat in their quarters and didn't know that they were actually free men.

Monterny regulated the controls of the simple air pressure chamber that prevented a too rapid exchange of air between the fortress and the atmosphere on Mars. Then they quickly passed through the tunnel they had burned out of rock to the hangar that was covered overhead with a thin wire mesh, camouflaged with moss and lichen.

The Supermutant herded the two men into the Z-35 where they manned the rayguns in the cockpit and at the aft end. He went into the little control compartment and closed the airlock.

There was nothing to hold him back now.

The engines began to hum, energy streamed through the conductors and activated the antigrav fields and the impulse drive. The ship vibrated slightly, rose up, retracted the telescopic landing supports and the bow broke through the camouflage net into the evening sky studded with stars.

The interceptor soared with maximum acceleration out into space, passed the relay ship Z-45 at a great distance and proceeded toward the asteroid belt that separated Jupiter from the inner planets of the Solar system.

This belt of small planetoids surrounded the Sun. Many of these planetary fragments were as small as a fist but there were also numerous bodies that were actual small worlds on which a ship could easily land and hide out. They trailed silently through the loneliness of space between Mars and Jupiter, circled the Sun once every two or three years and never returned to exactly the same place. On the other hand there were others that followed a circumscribed path which could be predicted precisely. Those were the larger asteroids with diameters of a hundred or more miles.

It would have been easy enough for Monterny to simply fly past the treacherous belt of fragments and return later to the plane of the planet. But the more hazardous way was also the shorter one. Moreover, an asylum on one of the moons of Jupiter seemed on second thought less secure. He was sure that his flight would be detected and the direction he took would similarly be noted so that it all obviously pointed to Jupiter as his goal. As a consequence of the high gravitation prevailing on the gigantic planet only one of the moons was practical for an extended stay. With the resources Rhodan had at his disposal it would not take long to trace him there.

By contrast, the asteroids were mostly unknown and only a few were charted in the stellar maps.

Clifford Monterny smirked when he passed the Z-45 on his right seven million miles away. He knew that the relay ship was not allowed to leave its station without orders and he felt reasonably safe. He assumed that its crew would notify Rhodan that the Supermutant had escaped in the direction of Jupiter. Rhodan would first have to check his abandoned place on Mars before he could embark on his pursuit. That would give Monterny enough time to find a new spot to hide on one of the passing planetoids. Once there he could switch off his engines and the most sensitive search instruments would be foiled by the ore contained in the rocks of the asteroids, making his detection impossible.

When the first of the small planets became visible in their reflected light far ahead of him, he reduced his speed. He was forced to find his way slowly through the maze of fragments.

Monterny lined the nose of his craft up against the general direction of the asteroids drifting toward him. He was not so foolish as to pick the closest asteroid where it would be easiest to find him. Little did he know that this was the mistake that decided his fate so tragically or he would have touched down on the first planetoid and gone into hiding.

No matter how potent Clifford Monterny was as hypno and telepath he was not endowed with the gift of infallible clairvoyance.

And thus he didn't know that turning into the path of the asteroid against the stream of the slowly drifting debris of an old planet would lead to his downfall.

*　　*　　*

The swearing Bell indulged in after a long fruitless search was too much for Tatjana. She operated the electronic instruments and the optical sensor. The door of the little radio room was open to the central control compartment. 'You ought to be ashamed of yourself, Mr. Bell, using such language! Isn't it enough if you just think it?'

'That'd be a total waste of effort,' Bell lectured her without taking his eyes off the frontal observation screen. 'If I swear it's for the sole purpose of relieving tensions and it works only when I speak. I've got to express it out loud if it's going to do me any good. As far as your tender ears are concerned, it would have been a useless sacrifice on my part to restrict myself to thinking without speaking for the simple reason that you're a telepath. You'd know all about my swearing, anyhow.'

Tatjana, who had listened incredulously to his lecture, shook her head. 'Thank you very much for taking the trouble to explain your behavior in such a logical manner. Since I'm a telepath I already knew what you intended to say.'

Pucky squatted as usual in a corner of the compartment and played with a dried-up carrot. He suspended it in the middle of the room and made it slowly sway back and forth with his telekinetic mental currents. When Bell made a grab for it, it slipped away with lightning speed and landed in the chair of the second pilot where it remained standing on end.

'The carrot is for eating, not playing,' Bell yelled with irritation at the mouse-beaver. 'You know I've strictly forbidden you to play such telekinetic games.'

'I'm practising,' Pucky tried to talk his way out, 'so that I can handle the Supermutant properly at the moment of decision.'

'I'd have liked it better if that buzzard hadn't have given us the slip. We've tried to depend too much on our instruments and on Tatjana's telepathy,' Bell nagged.

'I couldn't know that Monterny is able to screen his thoughts. The thought patterns of his two companions are also partially shut out by the hypnoblock. We'll have to wait for a lucky break.'

'I'm not blaming you, Tatjana. We're going to find him in any case if we follow him in the direction of Jupiter.'

'Or the asteroids,' Tatjana added.

'That's possible, too,' Bell admitted, looking out the window hatch where the Z-45 was visible at a distance. Lieutenant Bings had to leave his station in the orbit around Mars and escort Bell to take part in the search, since two ships could be more efficient than one alone. They kept in constant communication by UHF.

Bell slowly turned his head and looked at Tatjana. 'What did you say? Asteroids? Do you believe the Supermutant wants to hide out in the asteroids?'

'Why not? It wouldn't be such a bad idea.'

Bell had to agree. 'It might take us a long time to find him there.'

'Rhodan won't keep us waiting very long. With the search equipment of the Guppy we won't have much trouble finding the interceptor in the asteroid belt, regardless of how well he conceals himself.'

'H'm,' Bell was skeptical. 'Maybe we'll get lucky. I

believe in luck, it has always helped me in my life.'

'I'd prefer rather to depend on good search instruments and my own telepathy,' Tatjana replied and scanned the optical sensor. A wide panorama of the universe in front of the Z-13 moved across the picture screen with corresponding speed. The first of the larger asteroids rotated lazily in the feeble light of the Sun which stood at the rear of their ship. 'Monterny can't keep his thoughts shielded forever without expending himself completely. Perhaps he'll become careless when he sleeps.'

'You're also hoping for a little luck,' Bell gloated and grinned. 'Let's hope that we can corner him. That's all we can do. Rhodan has given us instructions merely to pursue him. He wants to take care of him personally.'

'I'll ...' Pucky began and shut up abruptly when he saw Bell's furious look. With an air of innocence he grinned with his big tooth and began to play with his beavertail. He seemed to have forgotten all about the carrot in the pilot seat. Bell noticed to his amazement that it was still standing on end as if held by an invisible hand. Was the mouse-beaver not only capable of telekinetically moving objects but keeping them immobile at a chosen spot for any length of time? Perhaps this was an ability of which he was not yet aware himself and that was only instinctively exercised by him. Bell decided not to say anything about it and to keep observing the phenomenon in secret. If his assumption were confirmed untold possibilities could open up.

Necessitated by the perilous proximity of the first

asteroids he turned his attention again to piloting his craft. One especially massive lump, at least thirty miles thick and irregularly shaped, sluggishly drifted clockwise around the Sun. It consisted of bare rocks and rugged gorges in which a little ship could easily disappear without being discovered.

Z-13 slackened its speed and so did the Z-45. Bell called the relay ship: 'Did you notice anything, Lieutenant Bings?'

'Nothing, sir,' the answer came promptly. 'A dead little world.'

'Nobody expected to find life on the asteroids,' Bell enlightened the Lieutenant. 'Go around the rock to the right. I'll meet you on the other side.'

The Z-45 complied without a word and veered to the side, disappearing behind the right horizon of the miniature world.

Bell descended till the cleft surface of the rocky planetoid was close below him and rolled along before his eyes like a relief map. Due to the lack of atmosphere each little detail was clearly recognizable. Nothing escaped the probing eyes of Bell.

Meanwhile Tatjana concentrated on any mental vibrations that might be present and tried to receive them. She was convinced she could sense the Supermutant if he were in close proximity and that it would not help him to shield his thoughts.

Pucky did nothing. He waited quietly for his chance.

Nobody was to be found on the mini-planet. To explore the depths of the spectacular gorges Bell would have had to land. But he was afraid to waste too much time. Therefore he gave the order to fly on when Lieutenant Bings emerged with the Z-45 over the short horizon and reported that his search was futile.

After the tenth attempt to catch up with the Supermutant on an asteroid, Bell groaned in disgust: 'As far as I know there are 50,000 of these rockpiles in our Solar system. If we want to comb them all we'll be old before we run into the Supermutant. Perhaps we're looking in the wrong direction.'

Tatjana shook her head. 'Clifford Monterny thinks logically and that's why he'll travel opposite to the direction of the moving asteroids, the same as we do.'

'Why would he do that?' Bell inquired.

'Because he can proceed at the slowest speed and let the fragments drift toward him. That way he'll require less time to find a refuge.'

Bell didn't quite agree with Tatjana that this was logical but he admitted that it could very well be true.

Without arguing the point further he aimed for the eleventh asteroid.

*　　　*　　　*

In the meantime a spherical spaceship touched down on the mesa back on Mars.

Major Deringhouse had insisted on personally leading the planned campaign against the lair of the Supermutant. He considered it his duty to make amends for the ignominious setback he had suffered.

There were several members of the Mutant Corps on board the *Good Hope VII* in addition to the regular crew of twenty-five men. It was André Noir's specific assignment to exorcise the spell of the Supermutant from the men still there. As they had already learned that Monterny had fled with only one ship, they could easily figure out how many of his men had remained on Mars.

Betty Toufry, the most potent of the telepaths, first established contact with Monterny's men. They were under a hypnoblock but there was no barrier to their thoughts and they were easy to read.

'They've been ordered to put up a defense,' Betty explained with a puzzled expression. 'Do you believe, Noir, that a senseless struggle can be avoided?'

The hypno shrugged his shoulders. 'Sengu will have to see where these people are waiting for us if they've already noticed our presence. Make sure that I work in the right direction. Then I'll try to break the block of the Supermutant. Have you been able to get in touch with the captured crew of our interceptors?'

'Their hypnoblock is fairly weak. Perhaps you ought to try to free them first. They should be able to help us later.'

Major Deringhouse left the ship together with Betty Toufry and André Noir.

* * *

Captain Berner and Lieutenant Hill sat in the control center of the Z-VIII-1 and whiled away the time with odd conversations. If an unsuspecting bystander could have listened in, he would have been greatly surprised.

'If these headaches persist much longer I'll be sure to go crazy,' Hill complained, putting his hand flat on his forehead. 'Perhaps I've lost my mind already.'

'It's the same with me,' Brenner chimed in. 'For instance, I can't understand why we're sitting here on Mars and waiting for something we don't know what. Until yesterday I felt a coercion as if somebody directed me and gave me his commands. Since last night this coercion is gone but headaches just like yours remain. I've got the feeling I could do what I want. But I don't feel like doing anything because I don't know what I want to do!'

Hill shook his head. 'Me too! And my men and yours the same. I know exactly how the Supermutant surprised us with his method called hypnoblock, if I'm not mistaken. We forgot to put on our absorber helmets. I know all about it but I don't have the strength to do anything to counteract it. It can't be right.'

'It's not right as far as the Supermutant is concerned but it isn't right with Rhodan either.'

'We must be mental hermaphrodities,' Hill exclaimed and started to laugh as if he had never heard a better joke. Berner remained calm. He didn't find what his companion had just said in the least funny. After awhile he touched his head and murmured: 'I believe the pressure's getting stronger and at the same time fading away. What's more I want to leave the ship now. I *must* leave the ship! Are you coming with me?'

Hill gave no answer. Silently Berner rose up led the way to the airlock where he donned an oxygen mask. The other men of the crew joined wordlessly.

None of them expressed any surprise when they found that the crew members of the other four interceptors had also left their ships and stood around in the ravine undecided what to do next. They all had evidently followed the same order that intruded from nowhere into their brains.

At the exit of the ravine three figures loomed up and approached slowly. Hill perceived with certainty that the orders came from one of the three people toward whom he walked together with all the other men.

'You're rid of the Supermutant,' he clearly understood in his brain. His headaches were suddenly gone. He seemed unfettered from a ring that had tightly been locked around his forehead and felt as if he could breathe freely for the firstime in days.

He quickened his step and knew all of a sudden that the insidious spell of the cunning Supermutant had completely subsided.

The all clustered around Major Deringhouse, André Noir and Betty Toufry.

'We hope you'll forgive us, sir, but ...'

'You don't have to tell me, Lieutenant,' Deringhouse interrupted him and smiled. 'I've been through the same experience. I even flew back to Earth and raised havoc on the territory of Terrania.' He noticed that Hill was horrified. 'I've been liberated by Noir just like you and he has given me back my life. At the same time we were able to gain possession of the most powerful destroyer the Supermutant had. He has fled toward Jupiter and is being pursued by us.'

Lieutenant Hill wanted to reply but never got the chance. Betty Toufry abruptly pushed Noir and Deringhouse to the side and threw herself flat on the ground. 'Take cover!' she shouted desperately. 'We're under attack!'

The men scattered apart and ducked behind rocks and protrusions. They had scarcely time to find cover when the firing commenced. Bullets whistled above their heads and ricocheted from the rocks.

André Noir rolled over next to Betty. 'Where's it all coming from?'

'From the left of the machinegun. They're planning to come out with their guns. Fortunately they don't have any rayguns, only small firearms. But we're completely defenseless. If you don't break the spell before their sally ...'

Noir ignored the exploding bullets and began to concentrate on the invisible gunners. It was an arduous feat to reach the fettered minds but once it was done everything went smoothly.

The shooting ceased.

Deringhouse and Hill remained in their prone positions like all the other men. Only Noir and Betty rose up without fear and walked toward the well-camouflaged machinegun nest. Not a shot was fired. Instead two, three figures emerged from behind the rocks, followed by others.

They were the defenders of Monterny's stronghold.

Their hypnoblocks crumbled away as Noir gave them the most intensive treatment and removed the last remnants of the evil will fostered upon them.

It would have been preposterous for anyone to claim that Clifford Monterny had selected the most valuable human stock. Rhodan had expressed no desire to recruit these men. They were to be taken back to Earth and delivered to their own governments. In the meantime they were given quarters in the *Good Hope VII* in a room they were forbidden to leave.

Now the last obstacle preventing radio communications had been removed and Deringhouse informed Rhodan of the events that had taken place and reported what they had found in the abandoned lair of the Supermutant. Then he asked for permission to establish contact with Bell. Rhodan did not hesitate long.

'I have some very urgent matters to settle. The negotiations between the governments concerning the contemplated One World Government have entered a decisive phase. I don't want to miss the next sessions under any circumstances. Moreover, I can't leave Ivan alone without supervision until I can be absolutely sure of him. Therefore I don't have any objections if you want to take part in the hunting down of the Supermutant. We must abolish the most terrible threat the Earth has ever known. If the Supermutant manages to lay low without being found, he'll come forth some day and profit from his experiences. Now he has been weakened and he is vulnerable. Monterny must be found!'

7 MONTERNY'S WORLD

The planetoid had no name and its orbit had not yet been described by man. It measured about fifty miles across and its shape resembled a cube. It displayed a remarkably rapid rotation and turned about its axis in less than an hour. The surface consisted of an agglomeration of precipitous cliffs and deep gorges which were continually shrouded in darkness. The higher peaks were illuminated at regular intervals by the far away Sun.

Due to the fact that new peaks were constantly coming into the range of sunlight and that the sight kept changing by the minute, it looked from a great distance like the perpetual flashing of a beacon.

This special circumstance was responsible for the turn of events.

First of all the blinking light attracted the attention of the Supermutant and increased his vigilance. Only after he magnified the picture of the asteroid on the observation screen did he find the explanation for the phenomenon. At the same time he decided to choose this planetoid as his temporary refuge. It would have defied explanation why he picked this one in particular.

He adjusted the speed of his interceptor to the velocity of the asteroid and began to circle around it. He saw with satisfaction that there were many good places to land. Even if one of Rhodan's ships were to fly over the asteroid it would be far from certain that he could be detected. And in case it really happened he still was equipped with excellent defensive armament and protected by the energy shield around the ship.

He quickly found a wide gorge with overhanging precipices.

The Supermutant was an outstanding pilot. He set the ship down in a smooth landing and waited calmly till the vibration of the hull was damped out. Then he ordered his two men to remain at their posts and to fire with their impulse-beamers at any ship that might show up. After that he went into the airlock, donned his spacesuit and left the interceptor.

Without knowing it he experienced what Bell always thought to have a special attraction: to float free and easy like a fish in water through a vacuum that was virtually without gravity. The Supermutant began to realize that there were other things besides wealth and power which made life worthwhile. He pushed off from the airlock and sailed across the valley, sinking ever so slowly. When he reached the rocky ground and made an imprudent movement, he soared aloft again like a feather in the wind almost up to the ledges at the top, to descend in tranquility to the bottom.

He forgot all about his precarious situation and felt deeply intoxicated. With a mighty leap he jumped up again and shot like a rocket into the star-studded sky. Naturally he followed the rotation of the asteroid and thus almost remained over the same spot while flying higher and higher, though loosing some of his speed.

Eventually he would reach the point where his levitation became insufficient to overcome the minute gravity that exerted its pull to bring him down in slow motion tempo.

At the apex he remembered the initial purpose of his excursion. He looked down but was unable to detect his ship. It was perfectly concealed by the cliffs jutting far out and no further camouflage was needed.

He waited serenely till he began to float down again. He was seized by a heretofore unknown majestic feeling of true freedom. He was unable to control the direction of his fall without using his hand raygun but this made little difference to him. There was plenty of space. He had a whole world to himself.

He consoled himself with the irony of fate. He always wanted to own the world – and finally a world was his. It was smaller than Earth and no life existed on it but it was a world that belonged to him and nobody would dispute it.

He landed gently on the ground of the valley, more than 1500 feet away from his ship. He cautiously bounced up at an angle and glided down in a parabola toward the interceptor, not rising more than thirty to sixty feet above the ground. He reached it with two leaps. The third one took him up to the entrance.

Here he remained for a moment to sort out his feelings and regain his composure. It was the firsttime he experienced such emotions. Floating weightlessly over a small uninhabited world had touched chords inside him that had never been plucked before. He almost lost sight of the reasons for his presence and the threatening pursuit of his deadly enemy.

At the rim of the gorge the light of the Sun crept like a living thing over the cliffs and fell into the shadowy depths, where it vanished. One hour later it would follow the same path and continue again and again.

For the firstime in his life the Supermutant saw how beautiful the world could be even in such bare and lifeless surroundings. His mind opened up and accepted the wonders that were presented to him.

And precisely at the same second he perceived a silent and merciless voice in his brain: 'Clifford Monterny, we've found you at last! Perhaps we'd never have caught up with you had you not become a human being in the end!'

The Supermutant shuddered. His brain-wave shield! He'd forgotten about it. Unrestrained, his thought-waves flowed out into space and a telepath had intercepted them. One of Rhodan's telepaths.

It was too late to remedy his oversight.

'Who are you?' he asked in his thoughts.

'Don't you recognize me? Tatjana Michalowna.'

To his sorrow the Supermutant realized that Rhodan had been so circumspect as to send a telepath after him who could not be influenced against her wishes. Tatjana was perfectly able to set up her insulation block and was sure to do so if it became necessary. But she probably had not come alone.

'So it's you, Tatjana. You've betrayed me. Aren't you satisfied yet? Do you want to kill me now? You're going too far!'

'Not at all, Supermutant. You can make your own choice how you want to die. Hurry up! We don't have any time to lose.'

It finally dawned on the Supermutant how his own victims must have suffered, now that he was on the receiving end. He was given an ultimatum that would result in his death. And why? Because for a short moment he had disdained power and ambition and had become a human being; because he had seen beauty in a ray of the Sun; in short because he had ceased being a monster for ten seconds.

Could it be that goodness was condemned to perish?

'I'm coming!' he said loudly and he knew that Tatjana understood him.

He took one last look at the inanimate world that had been his exclusive possession for a few minutes, turned slowly around and entered the airlock of the interceptor.

Silently the ordinarily heavy, here almost weightless, door closed behind him.

*   *   *

The steady blinking had attracted Bell's attention. Without interrupting his conversation with Major Deringhouse, who had come to help him with the *Good Hope VII* and requested a position check, he corrected the course of the Z-13 and made sure that the Z-45 followed him. 'So you'd like to participate in the hunt?' he asked while he tried eagerly to envision the source of the blinking. 'It'd be best if you'd take up the search in the opposite direction.'

'Why?' Deringhouse asked warily, knowing Bell only too well. 'Did you find a clue there?'

'No, nothing at all. Where are you located now?'

'About 120 million miles behind you.'

'Why don't you come here? Maybe you'll get here in time.'

Of course Bell couldn't know that his words would turn out to be only too true. He switched off the transceiver, gave Lieutenant Bings a few instructions and took the strange light effect under observation again.

When the Z-13 had come close enough to the asteroid Bell verified the true nature of the spectacle. He called himself a fool for not having recognized it earlier and ignored Tatjana's faint smile.

Tatjana engaged her 'telepathic receiver' again as they skimmed across the rugged suface of the asteroid.

And then she felt those bewildering thoughts infiltrate her brain.

At first she could scarcely believe that they emanated from the Supermutant inasmuch as they were good and even beautiful thoughts, most unlikely thoughts to spring from the mind of such a fiend. But then all her doubts were stilled.

The Supermutant was in the vicinity and the fantastic beauty of the sterile planetoid had touched him deeply. And because of it he had neglected to shield his thoughts.

'Clifford Monterny,' Tatjana said coldly, 'we've found you at last ...'

*   *   *

They waited at a distance from the asteroid. Lieutenant Bings in the Z-45 took up his position on the other side of the little satellite and maintained communication via telecom with Bell. In this manner it was impossible for the Supermutant to slip through in case he contemplated an attempt to escape.

Both men in the Z-45 put on their absorber helmets as Bell had done in the Z-13. Tatjana needed no artificial protection from the mental attacks of the Supermutant thanks to her inborn counteractive gift. Pucky was also able to screen his mind with a totally effective defense.

'How about locking you up?' Bell suggested jokingly. The mouse-beaver tried to make his trusting eyes glower menacingly. His tail quivered with excitement. 'I'd like to see you try it,' he taunted Bell, looking him up and down. 'Are you afraid I might take over the job of finishing off the Supermutant?'

'Nonsense!' Bell said, flying into a rage. 'When you get a whim to play you can cause a disaster. You can pilot the ship against my will and ...'

'There's nothing the Supermutant can do to me,' Pucky cut him short calmly. 'I've got more powers than you and Rhodan suspect.'

Bell shrugged his shoulders and turned his attention again to the rotating asteroid. The *Good Hope VII* was still too far away to share the action.

Suddenly Bell's head droned with a piercing pain. At first he believed it was some accident but peering at the telecom screen showing the interior of the Z-45 his worst fears were confirmed. Lieutenant Bings as well as Sergeant Adolf clearly exhibited symptoms of sudden nausea or head pains. Bing's eyes became glazed and fixed on some point out there in infinity.

'Tatjana!' Bell moaned with a last effort of his faltering will. 'The Supermutant! He's trying to ...'

The telepathic girl had already grasped what was

happening. Although she didn't suffer any of the ill effects that imposition of hypnoblocks always entailed, the telepathic commands of the Supermutant reached her as well but had no damaging results.

The ship of the Supermutant came into her view as it shot up with dizzying speed from the surface of the asteroid and turned into the opposite direction from the planetoid's trajectory. Evidently the Supermutant had no intention of losing time with the destruction of his adversaries. He continued fleeing to an unknown goal.

Bell sat paralyzed in his seat and did not react either when Tatjana yelled at him.

Pucky squatted in the corner as was his custom and grinned. He did it with so much mischievous pleasure that it would have infuriated Bell to the extreme if he could have seen it. But Bell no longer saw anything. His brain had been rendered inactive.

Pucky waddled forward and swung himself with a fancy leap into the seat of the copilot. He fastidiously removed the carrot that was still standing there and looked out the window. The ship of the escaping Supermutant was still clearly visible to the naked eye. It raced along the path of the drifting asteroids and threatened to immerse itself in the visible swarm of celestial bodies.

'By golly!' the mouse-beaver growled, narrowing his harmless-looking eyes with great concentration.

It was beyond his power to move the big mass of the Supermutant's interceptor but he was able to operate the controls by intensive concentration. However this would have been too strenuous for a longer duration.

Therefore he took recourse in a method that had already been proven twice before: he separated the two elements of the drive mechanism by teleportation and put the energy reactor out of working order. The interceptor continued streaking into the asteroid belt with the same tremendous velocity it had already attained.

Major Deringhouse paled when Tatjana called him.

'I can't get Bell out of the hypnoblock and I don't know how to fly this interceptor, nor can Pucky do it.' She described in a few words how Pucky had stepped into the breach, and concluded: 'You must get here as quickly as possible to prevent the Supermutant giving Bell orders against which I'd be powerless.'

'Your position?'

Tatjana gave him the information.

'O.K. I'll try a little hyperspace-jump. I'll be there in a minute.'

Hyperspace-jump!

Tatjana couldn't picture what it meant although she had heard of it. The ship slipped into the fifth dimension and materialized again at the target point in the fourth. The time factor was thereby completely eliminated.

Before Tatjana could think it through she saw the spacesphere pop up between herself and the Z-45, barely missing the asteroid. At first the stars became blurred in a circular section of the universe and then the *Good Hope VII* materialized again.

Soon the glazed look in Bell's eyes was restored to normal. His brain began to function again but he was unaware of what had happened. Tatjana brought him quickly up to date while André Noir in the *Good Hope*

VII brought Lieutenant Bings and Sergeant Adolf back to reality as well.

Pucky sat in the pilot seat and grinned happily. Bell glanced at him with a peculiar look and firmly gripped the controls of the Z-13 to perform a sharp curve veering in the direction of the Supermutant who had eluded him.

Spacesphere Z-VII and interceptor Z-45 trailed him closely.

'Is the Supermutant really unable to steer his ship?' Bell sought assurance from Pucky. The mouse-beaver nodded. 'And he can't accelerate either?'

'He has no energy left,' Pucky chirped. 'He'll be dead in a few hours when his air is gone.'

On the observation screen a point of light streaked rapidly through the slower asteroids. Bell magnified it and recognized the interceptor he was looking for.

Tatjana warned: 'It'd be senseless to go closer. If he sees us coming he'll try again to use his hypno-block ...'

Suddenly a brilliant light flashed far ahead.

Between the multitudinous specks of luminosity a small white sun flared up, then quickly burned out. When the eyes of the observers had become adjusted again to the accustomed darkness, the little point of light that had been the Supermutant's interceptor had vanished from the scene.

Bell increased his speed and slowed down again when he reached the tiny asteroid that had wandered into the fixed course of the disabled ship. It had a diameter of perhaps two miles and its mass was too big to be knocked out of its path by the smashing impact.

Silently it rolled on in its eternal orbit.

A huge crater had been gouged out of its surface. It still glowed.

Bell stared silently at the crematorium of the Supermutant. Tatjana, who had monitored the final few thoughts of the demoniacal fiend, murmured: 'His last wish has been fulfilled with ultimate irony: he wanted a world where he could rule alone and now he has found it. Nobody will ever contest the rulership of Monterny's World!'

Major Deringhouse spoke from the videoscreen: 'Well, this wraps up Operation Supermutant. And am I relieved. So will Rhodan be. We'd better advise him immediately so he can turn his attention to more worthy projects than a combat with a brutal fanatic trying to improve the world.'

'You mean imperil the world,' Bell murmured, correcting Deringhouse. 'Go ahead, report to Rhodan.' He studied the star map spread out before him. 'Take the Z-45 with you – I'll follow later.'

Deringhouse registered mild surprise. Tatjana also seemed puzzled. But Lieutenant Bings' interest suddenly perked up. A hopeful gleam came into his eyes.

Pucky munched his carrots. Any detour was A-OK with him.

'What do you have in mind?' Deringhouse finally queried Bell.

Bell winked confidentially at Bings on the other screen. 'I have to fulfill a promise I made to myself. The Supermutant is dead and I have something to do now. Have you ever seen a Venusian Palpitating Eye butterfly?'

'Huh! What's that?'

'You better take a course in e.-t. butterflyology,' Bell advised just as he switched off the telecom, thus failing to hear the happy cry of Lieutenant Bings, lepidopterophile extraordinary.

Z-13 whipped around and set course for the primeval planet.

Venusian Palpitating Eye butterfly, beware!